Ellis Peters ̶h̶a̶s̶ ̶w̶o̶n̶ ̶t̶h̶e̶ ̶C̶W̶A̶ ̶S̶i̶l̶v̶e̶r̶ ̶D̶a̶g̶g̶e̶r̶ for her crime novels, and ̶t̶h̶e̶ ̶S̶i̶l̶v̶e̶r̶ ̶D̶a̶g̶g̶e̶r̶ ̶f̶o̶r̶ *The Chronicles of Brother Cadfael*, now into their sixteenth volume.

The Piper on the Mountain

Ellis Peters

HEADLINE

ISBN 0 7472 3226 1

Printed and bound in Great Britain by
Collins, Glasgow

HEADLINE BOOK PUBLISHING PLC
Headline House
79 Great Titchfield Street
London W1P 7FN

CONTENTS

Chapter 1

THE MAN WHO FELL OFF A MOUNTAIN

Herbert Terrell went to spend his annual summer leave climbing on the Continent, and fell off a mountain in Slovakia. He was traversing a fairly steep rock face by a narrow path at the time, and it seemed that he must have missed his footing at a blind turn where the rock jutted abruptly. They found him fifty feet below, lying on a shelf at the foot of the slope. The shelf, being of white trias limestone, had predictably got the better of the collision. Terrell was impressively and conclusively dead.

Since there was nothing else they could well do for him, the local police did the obvious things. They took a long, cool look at the circumstances of his death, made a full report in the right quarter, popped the body in cold storage, and settled back to await instructions.

In due course, and through the appropriate channels, the news made its way back to all the interested parties in England; and between them, after their own fashion, they compiled Herbert Terrell's obituary.

::   ::

Sir Broughton Phelps, Director of the Marrion Research Institute, received the news on a Sunday morning in his London flat. Immaculate from church, he sat at his desk and ploughed his way with disfavour through the surplus of work that had kept him in town over a fine week-end, when he would very much rather have been in his garden in Berkshire, sunning himself in a lawn chair. However, he was a hard-working, serious minded and efficient public servant, very well aware of the responsibilities of his office, and the sacrifice of an occasional Sunday was something he accepted as part of the price of eminence.

For one moment, as he cradled the telephone, his whole mind was concentrated upon Herbert Terrell. He saw him more clearly than he had ever seen him in the flesh : forty-five or so, middling tall, even-featured, obstinately un-memorable; a useful, reliable subordinate, thorough, valu-able, arid and uninteresting. He saw again the dry, tough methodical body, the austere face, the humourless eyes. Can there be such a thing as a civil servant who has ceased to be anything separate from his office? Where the human qualities are feeble and ill-developed, perhaps the function eats them. Phelps saw his Chief Security Officer clearly as never before, but he saw him for only a moment. The features began to fade at once, until all that was left was the empty outline of a man, the vacancy that would have to be filled immediately.

The Marrion Research Institute was one of those hybrids so frequent in English public and social life. Old man Marrion had founded and endowed the place out of his oil millions, to prospect in dynamics and fuels for the future. The government had taken advantage of an optimistic director's over-spending to muscle in on this profitable field, and propped up the Institute's temporarily shaky finances in exchange for a watching brief and an option on all the re-sults the Marrion computers, drawing-boards and labora-tories produced. And this uneasy and contentious engage-ment had culminated in a slightly embittered marriage a year later, when the Ministry assumed the husband's role, and the Institute's scientists and mechanicians found them-selves islanded and fenced in by considerations of national security, who had ingenuously considered themselves, up to then, as dedicated to human advancement. They had felt, some of them, like the children of an autocratic Victorian household, strictly confined in a world where the cheerful and ungifted ran free. And some of them, Sir Broughton remembered, had rebelled. For a little while.

Circumstances had exalted Herbert Terrell's office, as circumstances had placed him in it. Where security pre-cautions are so tight and vital, the sudden death of one man cannot be allowed to disrupt essential services. To-day only a skeleton office staff and the maintenance men were in, to-morrow someone else must be securely installed in Terrell's place, that man-shaped outline, faint as a wraith now, solidly filled again, another hand on the curbs, another sharp eye on the most secret of secret files, the private personnel file.

He supposed he'd better contact the Minister, and ensure that his authority to appoint could not be questioned. The old man didn't care a damn, if the truth were told, but could be awkward if his perquisites were infringed or his nominal authority by-passed.

Sir Broughton Phelps picked up the telephone again, and switched on the scrambler before he asked for the number of the Minister's country house. No doubt where *he*'d be on a fine Sunday in July.

" Just a few minutes, darling," he said across the desk to his decorative and influential wife, who had put her head into the library to call him to lunch. " Something's come up unexpectedly. I won't be long."

She made a face at him, not entirely playfully. Not even on Sundays did his time belong to her, but she still considered that it should. " Something bad?"

"No, no," he said soothingly. "Nothing serious. Just a vacancy that's cropped up and has to be filled, that's all."

::   ::

The Minister's private secretary was a dashing young man whose native flippancy was held in check by his un-erring sense of occasion. He had more respect for Sir Broughton Phelps than for most people, but even that wasn't saying very much. He intended, however, to rise in his profession, and he was good at official languages. It didn't matter that Sir Broughton could disentangle his utter-ances at the other end of the line just as effectively as the scrambler could unscramble it. What is said, not what is meant, goes in the records.

" I'm extremely sorry, Sir Broughton, but the Minister's just gone out for some urgently needed air and exercise.

He's been hard at it all morning. Is it anything urgent? Should I try to find him? Or can I convey a message, and get him to call you back later?"

Fishing, thought Sir Broughton, mentally translating. Slept all morning, and won't come in until dusk. Could be over at Patterson's with his horses, but more likely fishing.

" I'd be obliged if you could get word to him. I just heard from Prague that the Institute's Security Officer has had an accident on holiday there, climbing in the mountains. I must make some arrangements to fill his place at once. No, it won't be a temporary appointment. Terrell's dead. If you could reach the Minister, I should be glad. My own nomination would be Blagrove, but of course I defer to his judgment."

The secretary unscrambled that into : What does the old devil care, as long as the job's done properly? Go and get his OK for me, and he can doze off again.

So he went. His thoughts, as he walked down the fields towards the river, were speculative and pleasurable. He had his eye on a certain promotion job himself, but unfortunately the most hazardous thing the present incumbent ever did was to play a moderate game of golf. A pity!

The Minister was flat on his tweedy back in the lush, vivid turf by the river, his rod carefully propped beside him. He opened one speedwell-blue eye, startlingly young under its thick grey brow, and trained it forbiddingly on his favourite assistant.

" No touts, no hawkers, no circulars!" he said, in the buoyant and daunting voice he had only acquired in his old age, after a lifetime of watching his step, and one liberating instant of abandoning every such anxiety.

"No, sir, I promise you needn't move. It's Phelps on the secret line. I wouldn't call what he has a problem. It could be a slight jolt. His right-hand man's died on him—Terrell, his Security Officer."

" Nonsense!" said the Minister, closing the eye again. "Terrell's out of England somewhere, the Caucasus, or some such outlandish region. Climbing. Does it every year.

Never could understand people taking up such unintellectual hobbies. What's in a lump of rock? What does he get out of it?"

"A broken neck, sir, apparently. It seems he fell off one of his pitches this time. They picked him up dead. No, sir, there's no doubt. Sir Broughton's had the official report. He's concerned about the vacancy, and would like your authority to appoint."

"Hmm, yes," owned the old man after a moment's thought, "I suppose we shall have to be thinking about that. Did for himself finally, did he? I always said it was an idiotic way of passing one's time. Why do they do these things? I take it Phelps has someone in mind for the job?"

"He mentioned one Blagrove, sir, if you approve."

"Old Roderick's boy. Might do worse. Used to work with Terrell before his promotion, I remember. All right, tell him he can go ahead, I approve." He closed both eyes again, and lay soaking in sun. Not fishing weather, of course, but you can't have everything. "Oh, and, Nick . . ." He opened one eye again, reluctantly.

"Sir?"

"There's a wife. Widow, rather. Terrell's, I mean. Seem to remember they separated, about a year ago. If Phelps knows where to contact her, perhaps he should break the news, otherwise they may have trouble locating her."

"Of course, I'll suggest it to him."

"Good boy!" said the Minister vaguely, and closed his eye again, this time with unmistakable finality, having taken care of everything. "Not that I think she'll be fearfully interested," he said honestly, and returned his mind gratefully to his own intellectual and productive hobby.

: :　　　　　　　　: :

Chloe Terrell, formerly Chloe Barber, born Chloe Bliss and soon to be Chloe Newcombe, turned her key in the door of her Chelsea flat about eleven o'clock that night, and heard the telephone buzzing at her querulously. She towed Paul Newcombe across the hall after her, and plunged upon the instrument eagerly. One of the most disarming things about her was that even at forty-three she still expected only pleasant surprises. Telegrams, sudden knocks on the door at late hours, letters in unknown hands from unknown places, all the things that make most people's blood run cold, merely made Chloe's eyes light up, and had her running to meet benevolent fortune half-way. Fortune, hypnotised like the audiences from whom she conjured applause simply by expecting it, seldom let her down.

"Oh, Sir Broughton—how very nice! Have you been calling me earlier? I'm so sorry! Such a lovely day, we ran out to Windsor."

She hoisted brows and shoulders at Newcombe across the pleasant, pastel-shaded room, to indicate that she couldn't make out what this caller could possibly want with her. Off-stage and on, her voice had made such a habit of intimacy that she never could remember to moderate the tone, whether for dukes or dustmen.

"Get yourself a drink, darling, and make yourself comfortable. One for me, too, please, and I'll be with you. . . ." The telephone clucked at her, and she took her smooth, cool palm from the mouthpiece again. "No! But *really?* Oh, no, it's impossible!"

She was a *belle laide*, brown, slender and sudden, with an oval, comical, elf's face, a blinding smile, and huge, purple-brown eyes. The eyes grew larger and larger now, dilating in pure astonishment, without, as yet, any suggestion of either consternation or delight. You would have been willing to hazard, however, that she enjoyed being astonished. A blazing smile touched her parted lips and lingered, but that could have been the reflex of disbelief.

"You've taken my breath away. I don't know what to say. Well, that's very understanding of them, and very kind. I think I *should* like to go out there, yes. I do think I ought to, don't you? Where was it you said? Just let me write it down." She scribbled indecipherably on the margin of the telephone directory, and whistled soundlessly at the outlandish spelling involved. "Thank you so much for letting me know, Sir Broughton, and for your sympathy. So kind of you! So very kind! Good-bye!"

She put down the receiver, and stood staring at Newcombe over it, wide-eyed, bright-eyed, open-mouthed.

" Paul, the maddest thing! Herbert's gone and got himself killed!"

Paul Newcombe spilled his whisky. A few drops flicked from his shaky fingers and spattered the large photograph of Chloe Bliss as Viola, which stood on top of the cabinet. She made a delicious boy.

"What did you say? Terrell *killed*?"

"Yes, darling! Had a fall, climbing somewhere in some impossible place." She spelled out from her own hieroglyphics, not without difficulty, and with a very engaging scowl: " Zbojská Dolina—can that be right, do you think? In something called the Low Tatras, in Slovakia. He'd worn out all the ordinary Alps, you know. He was quite good, so they said. But this time he fell off a traverse, or something. Anyhow, they picked him up dead."

"Look, honey, are you quite certain? Who came through with this? Can you rely on it that it's true?"

"Of course it's true. That was the head of his Institute on the line, and he had it officially. Poor old Herbert, who'd ever have thought it!"

"*Dead!* Well, I'm damned!"

"I know! And, darling, there's another thing, he says the Czechoslovak authorities are prepared to make it possible for me to go out there immediately, if I like, and see about the arrangements for bringing him home. Isn't that something? And I've never been to Czechoslovakia, so why not? After all, they've asked me. . . ."

"Chloe," he said, appalled, " you don't realise what this really means."

"Oh, yes, I do. But *I* didn't do it to him, you know. I didn't do a thing, it just happened. I can't make it unhappen. So what's the use of being hypocritical about it? In a way it's very convenient, you can't deny it. Now I shan't have to bother about trying to get him to agree to a divorce, we can get married whenever we like. And he did have a certain amount of money, besides being insured. Not that I'd have wished anything bad to happen to him just for that—or even at all. But why not admit to being interested in the results, now that it has happened? I hate humbug. Money's useful, and being a widow makes it easy to be your wife. And I want to be your wife, and you want me to—don't you?"

Newcombe put down his whisky, tilted her head back gently by a fistful of her thick, dark, straight hair, and kissed her vehemently. She emerged smiling.

" Well, then! And you will come with me to this place in Czechoslovakia?"

In a couple of weeks more he had, in any case, to undertake a protracted buying tour on the Continent—he manufactured and imported gloves, handbags, brief-cases and other small leather goods—but of course if she wanted him to he would go. She always got what she wanted out of him.

" Darling, this won't be business, not exactly. And I'll be there. It's fashionable to go behind the Iron Curtain this year, everybody's doing it. And it's the least we can do for poor old Herbert. The most, too," she added reflectively.

" I thought you hated humbug! Oh, all right, of course, if you want to go. . . ."

"Darling!" murmured Chloe, hugging him happily. " It'll be wonderful! I must get lots of beautiful black. I look well in black, and they're sure to be rather conventional in Central Europe. But I'll be a *fiancée*, as well as a widow! What superb timing!" She held him off for a brief instant to get a good look into his swarthy, self-confident, faintly wary face. " Are you sure you didn't pop over and *push* poor old Herbie off his mountain?"

He took it that she was playing games of fancy with him, and stopped her mouth the easiest and pleasantest way; but afterwards, on his way out, he had a queasy feeling that she might not have been joking. Either she was an immoderately silly woman with pockets of cleverness, as most people supposed, or she was an inordinately deep one who enjoyed appearing naïve. He could never quite make up his mind. Possibly she was both at the same time, or both in alternation. Whatever she was, she was irresistible, so he might as well give up speculating.

It was he who remembered, as he was leaving, that there was one more person who ought to be notified. The girl wasn't Terrell's daughter, of course, she belonged to Chloe's first marriage, and her father had been a quite distinguished scholar in his provincial way, Professor Henry Barber, the sort of middle-aged, shabby, eccentric, companionable wit for whom young and ambitious actresses fall with a resounding but transitory bang. He'd died when his daughter was twelve years old, which meant she was turned eighteen now. She hadn't, by all accounts, got on at all well with her first step-father. Took herself off to Oxford, so Chloe said, largely to get away from him; after old Barber's unpredictable and exciting vagaries, this one's cool, correct orthodoxy had infuriated her. Newcombe hoped profoundly that the second stepfather was going to be more of a success with her, but the thought of confronting a self-possessed and hypercritical eighteen-year-old frightened him more than he would have liked to admit.

" I suppose we ought to let Tossa know as soon as possible," he said. The " we " was partly a deliberate assumption of Chloe's responsibilities, and partly a pious prayer for harmony.

" Yes, of course, I'll call her in the morning. It's much too late to-night. *She*'ll take it in her stride," said Chloe sunnily. " She never could bear him."

: :   : :

Adrian Blagrove came back from his leave on Monday morning, clocked his mechanical way through the Marrion Institute's defences in depth, and reported prompt at nine to his own office in the secretariat. He had been there no more than three minutes when he was sent for to Sir Broughton Phelps's office in the most august and sacred recesses of Building One, and acquainted first with the fact of Herbert Terrell's demise, and then with the probability of his own permanent appointment to the vacancy thus created. Both pieces of information he received with the appropriate awe, gravity and gratification, nicely tempered with a modesty which was far from native to him. Bursting with health and lightness of heart after his fortnight's holiday, he felt capable of virtuoso performances. This job was what he had wanted for years. The frivolity with which he played his graceful little comedy of accepting it was entirely unconnected with the tenacity with which he would hold fast to it, and the intensity with which he would perform it.

"The appointment is at present temporary, pending confirmation. You understand that, of course."

"Of course!"

"But if you acquit yourself as well as I believe you will, I can say there's very little probability of confirmation being withheld. You've worked with Terrell, you know his methods and you know the organisation of his office. It's vital that someone shall be able to step straight into his shoes without a falter in the apparatus or its working. Can you do that?"

"I think I can. I'll do my best."

He was a lanky but graceful fellow, not as tall as he appeared, but marked everywhere by noticeable length; long hands, long feet, long neck, long face in the best aristocratic tradition. A little like a well-bred horse, but with certain indications that the horse was by a sire with intelligence out of a dam with devilment. He was forty-one, and still a bachelor, in itself a diplomatic achievement, especially in view of the social life he led, and the fact that he was, as the Minister had remarked, old Roderick's boy, and old Roderick's only boy, at that.

"Then you'd better move in at once, and take over. The secretariat is geared to carry your absence a week longer, by which time we shall have made a new appointment there. Well, good luck, Blagrove!"

"Thank you, sir!"

He left the presence very demurely. In the long, sound-less corridors of Building One he danced a little when there was no one else in sight, but it was a sarabande rather than a jig, and his face remained bland, intent and fierce with thoughtfulness. He knew exactly what he would do with the Security Office; he had had his own ideas ever since he had worked with Terrell on a certain dossier, and found the differences between their minds sharpening at every con-tact. It was that dossier, he remembered, that had put Terrell in charge of security at the Marrion in the first place.

He moved his own personal things into the office which had been Terrell's. Temporary the appointment might be, and pending confirmation, but Blagrove spent a coolly happy hour rearranging things to his liking, taking down Terrell's few mountain photographs from the walls, instal-ling his own yachting colour pictures in their place. The beautiful Chloe Bliss—he'd kept her picture in its place even when she left him—went into a desk drawer with the rest. Of Miss Theodosia Barber, Tossa to her friends and con-temporaries, there were no pictures, or he might have been tempted to secrete one for his own private pleasure when he had his predecessor's effects packed up for delivery to the widow.

By noon he had made a clean sweep. As far as the Marrion Research Institute was concerned, Herbert Terrell was not merely dead, but buried, too.

: :   : :

Chloe spent the whole of Monday shopping for glamorous mourning, and quite forgot about telephoning her daughter until late in the evening. While she waited for the operator to get the number of Tossa's Oxford digs she practised looking appropriately widowed and murmur-ing : " Poor Herbert !" There was a mirror suitably placed opposite the telephone for this exercise, so it wasn't time wasted. Shopping had acted as a tonic; she was looking blooming. Pathetically blooming, of course, but blooming. A pity about the name, though. What could you possibly do with " Herbert?" And yet how like him, how decorous and dull. Even death, even a sudden death like this, couldn't get such a name off the ground.

The telephone sputtered in her ear, and Tossa came on the line, sounding defensively grim, as usual. Unexpected calls at this hour of the evening could only be from home.

" Tossa Barber here. Mother?"

Where did the child get that gruff voice, like a self-conscious choirboy just stricken by puberty? She might make a hit on television some day, if she could learn to use her natural oddities, but she'd never make it on the stage. You couldn't fill a theatre with that bashful, suppressed baritone stammer.

" Darling, yes, of course it's me. Did I interrupt something for you?"

" No, nothing much, we were just planning this foreign route. And arguing a lot, of course. The boys want to drive and drive, they don't see any point in stopping at all, really. But it doesn't matter, once we're across to Le Touquet we can go wherever we like, and change the plans as much as we like. We've got the car, that's the main thing. It's a VW van, third-hand, but it's been looked after. And you won't have to worry about us at all, because we've got two first-class mechanics."

Trot out at speed all the mitigating circumstances, and pray that she isn't feeling maternal, or you've had it. Tossa and her fellow-students had been planning this holiday abroad all the term, and shelled out the money already for the air passage across the Channel, but one unpredictable impulse of mother-love on Chloe's part could still wreck it. Well, even if she quashed their plans, Tossa was determined she wouldn't go with her to Menton, to play chaperone for her and her next-man-in, before she'd even shucked off the present incumbent. She couldn't help it, and Tossa knew she couldn't, and didn't hold it against her. But, my God, how it complicated things!

" Tossa, love, there's something I've got to tell you.

Darling, I have to go abroad, very soon, to-morrow if we can get a passage. You must try to be brave for me. I know you can. It's Daddy. . . ."

Christ! thought Tossa, she *is* coming over all cosy and motherly. She can't have made it up with him? Even for her that would be an all-time, way-out crazy reaction. Even when she was gone on him she never tried this "Daddy" business before—never in life!

". . . something happened to him on holiday. He had an accident. He's dead, sweetheart!"

Never in life, no, just in death. That made sense, anyhow. Death called for a gesture, and Chloe Bliss wasn't the one to turn a deaf ear. Tossa stood frozen, clutching the receiver to her ear like some cosmic seashell bringing in the wavelengths of other worlds. And after a while she croaked faintly into the wood-dove's muted cooing: "You mean it? He's *dead*?"

"Yes, darling. He had a fall in the mountains, and was killed. Everybody's being terribly sweet to me, his chief rang me up himself to break the news, and the Czechoslovak authorities have offered to give immediate clearance if I want to go out and arrange about bringing him home myself. And I do think I ought to, don't you, dear? I've said yes, and Paul is arranging everything, and coming out there with me. I should feel so inadequate, alone. You do understand, darling? You mustn't let it spoil your holiday, you know, I shouldn't like that."

"No! I see," said Tossa numbly, and fumbled for the nearest available exit. "I'm sorry, Mother! It's quite a shock. How long do you think you'll be away?"

"Only a few days, I expect, maybe a week."

"And you don't mind if I go right ahead with this trip with Chris and the boys? It won't be immediately, there's ten days or more yet."

"Of course, go, darling. I know you'll be all right with Christine and her brother. Just take care, that's all I ask."

"Mother, I *am* sorry! About Mr. Terrell—Herbert. . . ."

There wasn't anything, not one single thing in the world, she could decently call him. The field between them had been as arid as that. And whose fault was it?

"Yes, sweet, I know you are. But there it is, these things happen, that's all. Now, promise me you'll get a proper sleep to-night, and not brood about anything?"

"No, I won't brood. You know we weren't close. I'm just sorry it had to happen to him. Mother, where *did* it happen?"

Chloe repeated punctiliously the names she had to spell out carefully each time from her own cramped handwriting. Zbojská Dolina, Nizké Tatry, Slovakia. Strange, far-off places. But not really so far-off, in these days of circling the globe, like Puck, in eighty minutes.

"I'll send you a postcard, darling. Now good night, and God bless! Don't stay up too late!"

"I won't, Mother. Good night! I'm terribly sorry!"

She was the first and last to say that about the death of Herbert Terrell, and mean it. She stood for a long time with her hand still pressing the telephone receiver down on its rest, and she knew what she had said for truth, but still she didn't know why. They had never come within touch of hands or minds, she and the dead man. He had been everything she hadn't been used to and couldn't get used to, precise, cold, methodical, thorough, pedestrian. He had courted her doggedly in ways that had only succeeded in alienating her still more implacably. But whose fault was it? Whose? A little more effort, no, a little more willingness, and she might have met him and achieved contact, she might have tapped unsuspected warmths in him. And now it was too late, he was dead. You couldn't make new discoveries about people when they were dead, and you couldn't make amends to them, either.

Well, no use dithering here like a wet hen, there was nothing she could do about him now. She marched back doggedly to her own bed-sitter, where her friends were sprawled happily over an outsize map of Europe spread out on the floor, the Mather twins in full cry. Tossa coiled herself once again in her place in the circle, and propped one elbow in the Aegean, and the other in the sea off Rimini. The soft, heavy wings of straight, dark hair swung forward and shadowed her face.

"Anybody interesting?" asked Christine, returning with capricious suddenness from Dubrovnik.

"No!" It came out so abruptly that it sounded like a snub, and she hastened to soften the effect, and made a mess of that, too. "Only my mother."

It was simply that she didn't want to talk about it, not yet, perhaps never. Think, yes, but talk, no. But to her own ears, and especially when she considered the fourth person present, who had never met her until this evening, it sounded distinctly ungracious, even a little shocking. Why did she have to be so maladroit? Chloe Bliss could and did put her foot in it right, left and centre, but always in the drollest and most disarming ways. Her daughter, it seemed, had to trip over everything, even the simple answer to a straight question. This friend of Toddy's wasn't going to find himself charmed or disarmed by rough cracks like that.

She cast a side glance at him from under the protective shadow of her hair. His name was Dominic Felse, and he was reading English literature. She didn't know much more about him, except that it seemed he was a useful man in a boat, and Toddy thought well of him. He came from some river town somewhere in the Midlands, where all the grammar schools crewed racing eights, fours and pairs as a matter of course, hence his prowess. He was in his first year, like herself, and probably within a couple of months the same age; rather tall and a little gawky still, with a bush of cropped, reddish-brown hair, hazel eyes that didn't miss much, and a fair skin that freckled heavily across the cheekbones and the nose. What he was thinking of her was more than she could guess.

His reaction, if she could have known it, was not one of shock, but of honest surprise. His own mother was a gay, sensible extrovert, who caused him nothing but pleasure, satisfaction and security, so all-pervading that it had never

even occurred to him to notice them at all. The revelation that this sullen, bright, brown imp of a girl had no
such serene relationship with her mother came as an eye-
opener, no matter how open eyes and mind had always
been, in theory, to the infinite variety of humankind.

She might, he conceded, studying her covertly as she
scowled down at Central Europe, be quite capable of con-
tributing her fair share to any friction that was hanging
around. He wasn't sure yet whether he was going to like
her, though any friend of the Mathers was practically
guaranteed in advance. But he was quite sure she was the
most delightful thing to look at that had come his way since
he'd arrived in Oxford.

Tossa would have been staggered to hear it. Brought up
on the legend of her mother's charm, she had never been
able to see anything in herself but the *laide*, and nothing at
all of the *belle*. That hadn't soured her, she had sighed and
accepted it as her fate. She had even convinced those of
her friends who had known her from childhood, like the
Mathers, that her view of herself was a true one. But you
can't fool a young man you are meeting for the first time,
without a preconception in his head about you, or any pre-
disposition to take you at your own valuation.

So Dominic Felse saw Tossa as *belle*, and not at all as
laide. Chloe's pale golden complexion became olive-bronze
in her daughter, and smoother than cream. Chloe's rounded
slenderness was refined in Tossa to the delicate, ardent tension of something built for racing, and anguished with its
own almost uncontainable energy. Tossa still was like a
coiled spring. It would be nice to teach her relaxation, but
it was nice to watch her quiver and vibrate, too. Her face
was a regular oval with wonderfully irregular features, lips
thoughtful and wry, so that you missed the sensitivity of
their moulding unless some sudden change in her caused
you to look more closely; huge, luminous, very dark brown
eyes. Her hair was a straight bob, just long enough to
curve in smoothly to touch her neck; very dark brown like
her eyes, heavy and soft and smooth, with a short, un-

fashionable fringe that left her olive forehead large and plaintive to view, an intelligent child's knotty, troubled forehead, braced squarely against a probably inimical world.

No, Dominic was in no doubt at all about Tossa, she was beautiful enough to stop any sane man in his tracks for another look, before she vanished and he lost his chance for ever. All the more effective because she didn't even know it. She might have a pretty good opinion of herself in other ways, for all he knew, but she hadn't the faintest notion that she was lovely to look at.

" She won't go and muck this trip up at the last moment, will she?" asked Christine, suddenly sitting bolt upright and abandoning the map, her grey eyes narrowing with suspicion.

Well, that was sound evidence, in its way. Christine had known Tossa's family almost since her infant school days.

"Oh, no, that's all right! She gave me her blessing. Don't worry about her, she's going abroad herself, anyhow." Tossa scowled even more fiercely, and stooped her weighted brow nearer to the map, only too plainly annoyed, thought Dominic, that she had volunteered something she needn't have volunteered. " How far did we get?"

"Oh, we needn't plan all that closely. As long as we've got all the papers we even *may* need, we can go where we like, and see how the time works out." Toddy drew up his long legs and hugged his knees. He was his sister's senior by an hour, and a good year ahead of the other two, and inevitably, or so it seemed to him, he was cast as the leader of the expedition. " Everybody's got valid passports, and I've applied for the insurance card. Anything else we need?"

Tossa stooped her head even lower towards the map. The heavy curtain of hair swung low and hid her cheek, drooping like a broken wing. She followed the west-east road through Nuremberg, and on towards the border, over the border and on through Pilsen and Prague, until the edge of the map brought her up short of the Slovak border, baulked of her objective. What was the use, anyhow? His death was an accident, and no fault of hers. If she'd somehow failed him, that was incurable now.

But if she'd only given him a chance to be liked! Not everybody can do that by warm instinct, most of us have to be helped.

She hadn't done much to help him, had she?

With a sense of wonder and disbelief, as if her mind had taken action without her will, she heard her own voice saying with careful casualness: " It wouldn't do any *harm* to have a carnet for the van, would it? Just in case we wanted to go farther afield? After all, we might—mightn't we?"

Chapter 2

THE MAN WHO WASN'T
SATISFIED

The person who was to put the cat fairly and squarely among the pigeons presented himself at the gatehouse of the Marrion Institute on a Thursday morning, just two days after Chloe Terrell and Paul Newcombe had flown to Prague. He was of an unexceptionable appearance, somewhere between twenty-five and thirty-five, and carried upon him the indefinable stamp of the public servant. The ex-sergeant-major in command of the Institute's blocking squad used towards him a manner one degree on the friendly side of his normal one, recognising him as one of *us*. That didn't help him, however, to penetrate even the outer defences.

He asked to see Sir Broughton Phelps, and in his innocence really seemed to expect to be haled through the barriers on sight. He would not state his business, except to stress that it was urgent. When he was told that no one got to see Sir Broughton without a Ministry permit, he adjusted promptly and without undue surprise to this check, but he did not go away, nor did he withdraw his demand. Instead, he asked if a message could be taken in to the Director or his Chief Security Officer, so that they might make up their own minds whether to see him or not. The ex-sergeant-major saw nothing against this; and the stranger scribbled a few words on his visiting-card, sealed it down in an envelope, in a way which might have been slightly offensive if he had not just had it impressed upon him how stringent security arrangements round here were, and handed it over.

The messenger delivered this billet to Adrian Blagrove's secretary, who preferred, understandably, to hand it over to his chief unopened. So it happened that Blagrove was the first to withdraw the card and read what the stranger had written.

Robert Bencroft Welland (said the card)
Assistant Commercial Secretary
British Embassy, Prague I,
Thunovská 14,
CSSR.

And above the name was scribbled in a vehement, cornery hand:
Terrell's accident was no accident.
:: ::

Robert Bencroft Welland came in gravely, displaying no signs of elation at having penetrated the first protective layers, and no haste about completing the feat. He accepted a chair and a cigarette, and settled his brief-case conveniently on the carpet beside his feet. Shut in together, they contemplated each other across the desk which had been Terrell's.

"Mr. Welland," began Blagrove very soberly, "you appear to be suggesting something which doesn't seem to have occurred to anyone else, even as a possibility. The Slovak police were quite satisfied of the facts of poor Terrell's case, and made very full and correct reports which apparently convinced our authorities just as completely. I take it this is an unofficial approach, or you would have been sent here already provided with the means of reaching me, and wouldn't have had to write me—this little billet." It glanced coyly between his closed fingers for an instant, and vanished again. "May I ask if you've confided your doubts to anyone in Prague? Any of your superiors?"

"No, I haven't. I came to the Marrion Institute because it seemed to be the party most affected by Terrell's death, and what I believe to be the facts about it. I came over only yesterday, on a week of my leave, and I had some enquiries to make before I was ready to come to you."

"Presumably, since you're here," said Blagrove drily, "your enquiries produced positive results. You realise you're the *only* person who has questioned the circumstances of Terrell's accident?"

"I could hardly let that influence me, could I?" said the young man mildly, with such simplicity that Blagrove took another and closer look at him. Under thirty, probably, of medium height and lightly built, neat, tow-coloured hair, all very presentable, all very ordinary. Put him among an office-full of civil servants, and you could lose him in a moment. Except that the good-natured face, earnest and dutiful to the point of caricature, had a little too much jaw for comfort, and confronted his seniors with a pair of wide-set blue eyes of startling directness and obstinacy. He looked, at first glance, like all the others of his class and profession; but at second glance it was clear that being on his own wouldn't stop him from doing whatever he felt he had to do.

"Perhaps," suggested Blagrove carefully, "you'd better tell me just why you're not satisfied."

"In the first place, because I knew Terrell, and I've seen the place where he was found. Oh, I didn't know him well, but it so happens I've climbed with him, last year in the Zillertal, so I know his class. He was an excellent climber, on a rope or alone. The Zillertaler Alps were his proper league. But the Low Tatras, where he was found, are walking country. Not alpine stuff at all, but open, grassy slopes and rounded summits, with wooded valleys. You could find a few practice pitches there, rock outcrops, scrambles, that kind of thing. But nothing to tempt a man like Terrell. So the first question, even if I'd known nothing more, is: "*What was he doing there at all?*"

"I see nothing to prevent even a climbing man from fancying a walking holiday now and again, for a change," objected Blagrove reasonably.

"Nothing whatever. Except that they just don't do it. Hardly any of them, and certainly not Terrell. Once you're as proficient as he was, you lose interest in the mild stuff. The climbs have to get harder all the time, and higher. Failing that, you just go somewhere new, where at least they're different, unknown. But you don't go back to walking and scrambling. And for that matter, even if you did go back, you certainly wouldn't fall off a perfectly good traverse path, even at a blind corner, like the place where they found him."

"I shouldn't like to be so sure it couldn't happen. The skilled and experienced sometimes fail to give all their attention to the easy bits." Blagrove was playing somewhat irritably with the card he held in his fingers. "Unless you have something more than that to go on. . . ."

"Oh, I have. You see, Terrell got in touch with me early this year, and asked my advice about good climbing country in the *High* Tatras. You don't know that part of the world? There's this great, open valley of the river Váh, running east-west, and to the south of it these broad, rolling crests of the Low Tatras. Then to the north, sickle-shaped, like this, and much more concentrated, there's the cluster of the High Tatras, the highest peaks in the whole Carpathian range. *These* are for climbers. Anything up to nearly nine thousand feet, granite, three hundred or so peaks packed into about fifteen miles length, and magnificent country. I advised him to book in at Strba Lake, or at Tatranská Lomnice. And he did. He booked for two weeks at the lake. So what was he doing across the Váh valley in the *Low* Tatras?"

Blagrove raised his brows. "He could surely have changed his mind. How do you know he went ahead with his booking?"

"For the best reason in the world," said Welland flatly. "Because *I* made the reservation for him, as long ago as April. And I know he turned up on time at the hotel, because he dropped me a card on arrival. He said nothing then about moving. On the contrary, he confirmed the arrangement we'd made by letter earlier. I was supposed to go along and spend the week-end climbing with him on Kriván. Only, you see, before the week-end came we got the news at the embassy that he'd been found dead—fifty kilometres away across the valley, in the Low Tatras, where he'd never intended going. He'd checked out from Strba Lake on the third day, and gone away to a small inn in one of the valleys in the other range. No mystery about *what* he did, up to that point. The only mystery is *why*?"

"And you think," said Blagrove, his hands still and alert before him on the desk, "that you know why?"

"No, not yet. All I have is certain indications that may suggest reasons. As, for instance, that at some time after his arrival at the lake, something happened within his knowledge, something that caused him to pay his bill there and then, and go rushing off across the valley. No one at the hotel could account for it. He just left. But something happened that made him leave. If it had been simply something that disinclined him to stay where he was, made him dislike the place or feel uncomfortable there, he'd most probably have transferred to another hotel, somewhere along the range, or come back to Prague. Instead, he made his way for some reason to this one particular valley in the Low Tatras, not even a very frequented place. Whatever it was that happened didn't just drive him away from Strba Lake—it led him to Zbojská Dolina. And believe me, it can have had nothing to do with climbing. Do I interest you, Mr. Blagrove?"

"You interest me, yes, up to a point. You didn't say any of this to your superiors in Prague?"

"No, I didn't. One doesn't like to start hares of that kind without making sure first of as many facts as possible. I had some leave to come, and I used it to come over here. Whatever drew Terrell to the Low Tatras, it can't have been something private and personal from his own past, because he had no connections there, this was his first visit. He knew nothing of the country, he knew none of the people. I thought, knowing what his work was, and what it might sometimes involve, that there might be a link with something he'd handled or known about in the course of his duty. I hoped to get an interview with his widow, but she wasn't in when I called at her flat."

"She's in Slovakia at this moment," said Blagrove, "seeing about having her husband brought home."

"Ah, so that's it, I see. Well, since I could get nothing from her I spent the afternoon and evening among the press files, going back over the details—only the published details that are open to everybody, of course, but you'd be surprised how much that covers—the details of any reportable work handled by Terrell during the last few years. I have friends among the pressmen. I didn't tell them what I wanted, I didn't know myself. I just picked over their memories and then worked backwards through the files. I thought somewhere there must be something to dig up, something that would tie in at one end to Terrell, and at the other end to Slovakia—with a lot of luck, even to that part of Slovakia."

Blagrove let out his breath in a soft, cautious hiss, and braced his shoulders against the back of his chair. "And you found something?"

"I found," said Welland with deliberation, "the unfinished case of Charles Alder."

In the moment of silence they stared steadily at each other.

" Or of course," said Welland, " if you prefer it, the case of Karol Alda."

It was a pity. It was really a pity. To have the whole affair tucked away peacefully in its coffin as an accident would have been so much simpler and more satisfactory; but there were two good reasons for abandoning, here and now, any attempt to dissuade this young man from pursuing his enquiries further. First, he wouldn't be dissuaded; the supererogatory jaw was set, and the uncompromising eyes expected and would countenance only a zeal for justice the equal of his own. And second, to assume the responsibility for smothering a matter as serious as this was too great a risk. It would have to go to higher authority, however vexatious the results might be.

" I think," said Adrian Blagrove, pushing back his chair, " I really think you'd better come with me to the Director, and tell him the whole story."

: :   : :

Sir Broughton Phelps sat forward at his desk with his lean jaw propped broodingly on a closed fist, and scarcely took his eyes from the visitor's face as Welland repeated the tale of his reservations and his discoveries, until he reached Charles Alder's name.

There was an expectant pause there. Welland looked a little pale and a little anxious when it prolonged itself beyond his expectations. He would have liked someone else to contribute something, a hint of appreciation, or at least belief; better still, a grain of confirmation. But when no one obliged, he did not look any the less convinced or any the less obstinate.

" I know you must be much better informed than I am, sir, about this case of Alder's. But if you want me to sum up everything as I find it, I'll willingly go on."

" Please do," said the Director, fingering the clipped silvery hair at his temple. " I assure you you have my very serious attention."

"What I found, of course, was the dossier—or the published part of it—compiled by Terrell after Alder's disappearance. Otherwise I wasn't conscious of ever having heard of the man before. So my information comes, virtually, from Terrell himself. Alder was a refugee who came over here with his parents in 1940, and settled in England. He was then fifteen years old, and already something of an infant prodigy, musically and mathematically. I believe they often go together. His father was a physicist, and after a probationary period he was allowed to work here. He proved valuable, and before the end of the war all three of them were naturalised. The boy had studied physics, too, but soon began to distinguish himself in his own special fields, as composer and performer, and in the world of pure mathematics. Perhaps he was even a genius. After the war he did quite a lot of experimental flying, and originated some minor improvements in aircraft, ending up in this Institute, where he was associated with a number of important modifications in aircraft and car design. Also, it seems, he sometimes had differences with the government and his superiors. He objected to the exclusively military use of innovations which he seems to have considered could be beneficial in civil life. And he didn't like techniques of his evolving to be kept under wraps, when he believed they could be adapted to help with necessary processes in underdeveloped countries. He seems to have been a difficult colleague of individual views, insubordinate, unwilling to conform against his judgment. And he must have been really brilliant, because according to a *Guardian* article I found, about the time he vanished he was definitely in the running for the directorship of this Institute, and at his age that was fantastic." The young man raised his direct and daunting eyes, and looked the present Director full in the face. "Can you confirm that, sir?"

"I can and I do." Phelps committed himself without hesitation. "The man was brilliant. He was a computer that thought and reasoned. No programming, no minding, no servicing necessary. We spend millions trying to construct an Alder, and then wear out bright young men feeding it. When we get a genuine one as a free gift from heaven we usually fail to recognise him. But difficult he certainly was. Go on, finish your exposition."

"Finally, after both his parents were dead, Alder wished and offered to resign from here. I don't know exactly why, I suppose he was disturbed by a feeling of alienation from the aims of this place, and maybe he felt out of sympathy with policy in general. Anyhow, he was obviously valuable, and he was persuaded to think it over while he took some leave that was due him. I take it the authorities here hoped he would change his mind and stay on. He went off into Savoy alone. And he never came back.

"When he failed to return on time, there were rumours and an alarm, and Terrell was sent to France to follow up his tracks, until they ended without further trace in Dauphiné. It was automatically assumed that he'd departed behind the Iron Curtain, but no more was ever heard of him from any quarter. He *could* have come to grief somewhere in the mountains, being alone there. But the obvious inference was that he'd turned traitor. And Terrell was the man who followed up his case, and compiled a very damning dossier out of all those small unorthodoxies in Alder's professional life and attitudes. I'd say that that dossier made it impossible for him ever to come back—supposing, of course, that he'd wanted to change his mind."

"Happily we have no reason to suppose anything of the kind," said the Director tartly. "You don't seem to have wasted your time, Mr. Welland. You find all this relevant?"

"I think it becomes very relevant, sir, when you remember that Charles Alder was born Karol Alda, of a Czech father and a Slovak mother. Especially when you add to that the fact that the mother's birth was registered at Liptovsky Mikulás, not twenty miles from Zbojská Dolina."

"Let me understand you clearly. You are suggesting, I take it, that Alda may be there in those parts now—that he may have gone back to his old country and his old allegiance?"

"I am suggesting that it is more than a possibility. I should also hazard that that is exactly what you must have believed he would do."

"And you'd be right, naturally. But the fact remains that there has never been any indication, not the slightest hint, that he did so." He got up abruptly from his desk and began to walk the room, not restlessly, but with a controlled, energetic step, like a man starved of proper exercise making the most of cramped quarters. The two younger men followed his pacing with alert eyes, and waited. "You think Terrell may actually have *seen* Alda?"

"Something unexpected happened to him, something that drew him across the river valley to Zbojská Dolina. It could be connected with Alda. I don't claim more than that."

"But you imagine more, much more. You think, don't you, that either he saw Alda, or picked up somehow a clue to his whereabouts? And that he followed it up, and got himself pushed off a mountainside when he got too close for comfort. That's what you think, isn't it?"

Welland paled a little at seeing it posed before him in this pointblank fashion; even he had a trace of the diplomat's dislike of formulating anything too exactly. But he stared back gallantly, and said emphatically: "Yes."

Blagrove stirred protestingly. "But, good lord, the case is six years old now! It's no longer important. Times have changed, the cold war's a dead issue, or dying, trade's developing. Even if Terrell did turn up unexpectedly on his trail, why should Alda even care any more? Neither Terrell nor any of us could be any threat to him there. And would it be worth killing the man just for plain spite?"

"But isn't that missing the point of what Sir Broughton said a minute ago?" argued Welland intently. "You expected him to turn up in Czechoslovakia. Word of where they are always leaks out eventually, doesn't it? But not a word ever leaked out about Alda. So wherever he is, secrecy is vital—to him, and to whoever is cashing in on his work now. Six years of successful concealment argues it's important enough to murder for. I believe there's something going on right now, right there in the Low Tatras, that has to be kept absolutely secret, and that Alda is at the heart of it. I believe Terrell found out, or they thought he had found out, what he couldn't be allowed to report."

" If there is anything in this," began Phelps, after a long and pregnant pause, " and I'm not admitting yet that there necessarily is, but *if* there is—then you realise it's happened in a place and in circumstances which practically put it out of our power to investigate. If he *is* there, and if he is being kept as tightly wrapped as all that, then we must assume that this is national business. In which case we must also assume that the Czech authorities, if not the police on the spot, know all there is to be known about this death."

" I'm convinced," said Welland vehemently, " that they do. The local police know about mountains, they can't have failed to see what a queer sort of accident it was for an experienced man. Yet within a day they'd closed the case. I think they've had their orders."

" Even if you believed in their honesty," said the Director drily, " our position would be the same. I can't impress upon you too strongly, Mr. Welland, that everything to do with this Institute is top secret. In this case or any case that involves us in any way, nothing whatever may be confided to foreign authorities, friendly or otherwise. There can be *no* overt enquiries."

"No, sir, I realise that. But I'm there on the spot. I week-end in the mountains quite frequently, they're used to me. I move about quite freely, I speak the language a little. I could look into it myself, without alerting anyone."

He offered them a dutiful silence, but neither of them, it seemed, had anything to say. They looked at him narrowly, with unwinking concentration, and he found it unnerving that he had not the least idea what either of them was thinking. They were the product of the closed establishment, closed men, each in his own air-tight, suspicious, ambitious, narrow world, specialising in ever more attenuated expertise. The horrific thought visited him that he might live to be like them. He found it absolutely vital to give utterance again to the realities that still existed in him, while they existed.

" I intend to find out if Terrell was murdered. I can't help it. If he was killed for activities that seemed to him in line of duty, then I believe we owe it to him to investigate, and to see that justice is done. He's entitled to justice. Quite apart from the possibility that something is going on there that affects our national interests and security. We can't just let murder go by default. It isn't right."

He produced this final simplicity with an authority that restored its lustre. He said with dignity : " I would much rather proceed with your approval, of course. I hope I have it."

But he would proceed with or without it. He was committed by his conscience. An interesting survival, but there he was in the flesh, determined and distressed, perfectly conscious of what he was saying and doing, and prepared to be judged by it.

" My dear boy!" said Sir Broughton, for the first time warming into the charming smile that tansformed his professionally austere face into something human and likeable. " Proceed with our blessing, of course, but with our warnings, too. One man, according to your theory, has already been killed. I beg you to take care of yourself. That's the first essential. The second is the preservation of complete secrecy for this establishment. That I can't over-stress. And the third thing is something I feel I ought to tell you. If you're going into this at all, you must go with your eyes open. Nobody knows this, outside this Institute and its parent Ministry."

He came back slowly to his desk, and leaned on his hands there, pondering. For a moment he looked more than his age, an elderly man bowed by his responsibilities.

" When Charles Alder vanished, his current working

notebooks vanished with him. They contained all his projects at the experimental stage, and at that stage they were
so completely his own brain-children that no one could continue his work on them. No other sketches, no other outlines
existed. We don't know, apart from a few preliminary
ideas, what was in them. But he was at the height of his
powers, and working like a demon, mainly on problems of
aerodynamics. If he's been pursuing the same lines of research elsewhere, there could be sensational developments.
There could be more than enough at stake to invoke
murder. You understand that?"

"Yes, sir," said Welland, weak with relief and gratitude,
"I understand."

"And you understand the absolute need for secrecy?
You must not say one word to anyone about this. You
haven't taken anyone into your confidence? The press men,
your friends?"

"I didn't tell them anything, beyond showing curiosity
over Terrell's record. Knowing I'm stationed in Prague,
they wouldn't wonder at that." He was all eagerness now,
dazzled and exhilarated by the Director's energy.

"And no one else, either?"

If Welland hesitated at all, it was so briefly that the instant passed unnoticed. "No, sir, no one knows anything
about this from me."

"Good! Then go ahead, but take care of yourself. If
you do hit upon a lead to Alda, you must report at once to
us. Don't go on alone and take risks, just report back and
wait for orders, you understand? I'll see that the Minister
is kept informed, otherwise no one must know of this except
the three of us here. I'll arrange with the embassy in
Prague, and have any message from you transmitted direct
to us here by telephone. We'll have a code signal agreed
before you leave here. If you locate Alda, then send it.
When we receive it, it may be advisable for Mr. Blagrove
to come to Prague on some pretext, to be on hand—and to
help you," he said, the human smile reappearing for one

abstracted instant, "in case of need. Even you may need help sometimes, Mr. Welland. Who knows?"

" I'll be very careful, sir. You can rely on me."

" We are relying on you, my boy. You'll report to nobody else but this Institute. Not even our people in Prague. You understand? *Nobody* else!"

He had accomplished all and more than he had hoped for. At the edge of an adventure, with the water cold and mysterious before his plunge, Robert Welland was a vindicated, even a happy, man.

Or he would have been happy, but for one small scruple.

   : :   : :

As soon as he left the conference in Sir Broughton's room he hurried to the Underground station, and made his way back into London, to the Chelsea street where Chloe Terrell had her top-floor flat. It hadn't, of course, been absolutely honest of him not to tell Sir Broughton about the note he'd dropped through Mrs. Terrell's letter-box, when he found her out. The note certainly did confide something, more than he should have said, even to the suggestion of murder. But there was no harm done, after all, because Mrs. Terrell was not merely away from home, but out of the country. He had Blagrove's own word for that. So no one would have read the note he should never have been so indiscreet as to write, and what he had said was not, in fact, a lie. No one knew anything about this affair from him. And no one would.

There wasn't even any hurry about it, his sense of anxiety and impatience was folly. She was in Czechoslovakia, and she wouldn't, couldn't be back yet. He had plenty of time to dig out the porter of the service flats, explain that he'd left a vital paper by mistake, not knowing Mrs. Terrell was out of the country, and must recover it and get word to her elsewhere at once. The porter would have keys, and it wouldn't be difficult to establish his own good faith. When he'd burned that note he would feel better, because his shadow of a lie wouldn't exist, then, and there would be no leakages through him. He liked to have everything above-board, and that was how it would be.

All the same, his mind was not quite easy. Better just have a look at the top-floor flat first, before he tackled the porter, and make sure that it was still closed and empty. Just to reassure himself.

The lift was creaking its way slowly upward as he stood in the hall; he had caught a glimpse of the door closing upon a dark, slender girl with her arms full of parcels, and to judge by the time that elapsed before the lift-cable was still and the door clashed open, high up the shaft, she was disentangling her purchases at least four floors up. He pressed the call button, and nothing whatever happened. A woman with both hands full doesn't stop to close the lift doors after her. He would have to walk up.

He didn't know why he was hurrying as he tackled the stairs. Hadn't he already told himself that there was no haste, no possibility that Mrs. Terrell would have returned and read his note? But he began taking the steps two at a time before he reached the second landing, and by the fourth he was running, his heart pounding and his breath short. He came to the corner from which he could see Chloe Terrell's door, and baulked as if he had run his nose into a brick wall. For the outside door of the flat stood open. And the pretty girl with the parcels stood in the hall with her burdens dropped unceremoniously about her feet, and his letter open and unfolded in her hands.

She was still as a statue until his rush of movement ended in abrupt stillness, and then she was aware of him, and looked up at him over the spread sheet of paper with great dark eyes blank with horror. For a moment they stared at each other in fascination and dread. He didn't know what to say to her. He didn't know what to think.

She couldn't possibly be, she wasn't more than eighteen or nineteen! But women did marry as young as that. How was he to know that the wife would be a mere child? Horrified, he lifted his leaden feet up the last few steps, and

moved towards her like a hypnotised rabbit, utterly helpless.
"Mrs. Terrell. . . .?"

She stared back at him as if she had heard nothing, following her own fixed channel of consciousness. She looked
down at the sheet of paper in her hand, and back at him.

"You're Robert Welland? It was you who left this
note?"

She had a voice that startled, an octave deeper than anyone would have expected; a gruff whisper, like an adoles-
cent boy not yet used to his new instrument. She took a
small step back from him, warily and wildly, and stumbled
over her own parcels discarded on the floor.

"Yes, I'm Robert Welland. I didn't mean. . . . I didn't
realise. . . . Mrs. Terrell, I must apologise and explain. . . ."

"I'm not Mrs. Terrell," said the girl, shrinking. "I
shouldn't have opened it, but I thought it might be something I ought to send on. I'm Tossa Barber. Sorry, that
won't mean a thing to you." She put up her hand dazedly,
and pushed back the fall of dark hair from her brow. "I'm
Mrs. Terrell's daughter. I came up to do some shopping for
the holidays, and I use her flat when I'm in town." It was
extraordinary that she should feel she had to explain to him,
when it was he who had so much to explain, the letter, the
implications of the letter, his presence here in such a hurry.
Suddenly she was calm for both of them, because it was too
late to take back anything, and there was no way to go except forward. "You say here," she challenged pointblank,
"that my step-father was murdered."

In what he had written he had not, he remembered, used
that word. He thought of a hundred ingenious evasions, and
confronted by Tossa's large, unwavering eyes, rejected them
all. "Yes," he said helplessly, "that's what I believe."

"Come in," said Tossa. "You may as well. Now I have
to know. You can see that, can't you? I've *got* to know."

He made one convulsive attempt to extricate himself, even
as he was stepping forward into the flat and closing the
outer door behind him. He couldn't possibly confide in a
child like this, even if he hadn't just sworn secrecy under

awful warnings; but neither could he stand in an open doorway close to the echoing well of the stairs and the lift-shaft, and make his excuses for all the house to hear.

"Miss Barber, I'm very sorry I've alarmed you for nothing. Since I left this note for your mother I've had an opportunity to consult the people who're best-informed about your father's . . ." These relationships were confusing him, he didn't quite know where he was with them. "——about Mr. Terrell's death. I should be glad if you would try to forget about the whole matter. I did have my suspicions, but they're not shared by others who should know best, and it may be that I was quite wrong."

"You just said: 'That's what I believe'," she reminded him, "not: 'That's what I *believed*'." She slipped by him very quickly at the slight movement of retreat he made, and put her back against the door. "No, you can't! You can't go away now and leave me like this."

And he saw that he couldn't. Not simply because she already understood too much, and could make his escape impossible, but because her face was so desperately resolute and her eyes so full of an acute personal distress for which he was responsible. It was already too late to undo that; all his disclaimers wouldn't convince her now, all his reassurances wouldn't restore her peace of mind. His own little indiscretion had trapped him. It wasn't enough even to plead that he had promised secrecy, since his promise had been breached by accident almost as soon as he had given it.

"Miss Barber," he began earnestly, "I did come here with certain information that disquieted me, and I wanted to consult Mrs. Terrell before I took the matter any further. I've now had it impressed upon me that this whole affair is urgently secret, and I'm bound by that. It was foolish of me not to have realised it for myself, and I'm deeply sorry that my mistake has now caused you distress. I wish I could undo it."

"You can't," said Tossa fiercely, "and you can't leave it like that. Maybe I shouldn't have read it, but I did, and he was my step-father, even if we weren't at all close, and do you expect me just to sit back and live with the thought that somebody murdered him, and not do anything at all about it?"

"I sincerely hope there's going to be no need for *you* to do anything about it. That's a job for others."

"No!" she protested passionately. "That isn't good enough. That doesn't help me."

He had already reached the point of knowing that he was going to tell her everything. Maybe he was a good judge of human nature, and maybe he wasn't, but it seemed to him that there was only one way of ensuring that secrecy should indeed be complete. She had the passion to demand her rights from him, maybe she had also the generosity to meet him half-way when he piled the lot into her arms without reserve.

"Miss Barber, I gave my word. There's no way I can satisfy you, except by extending that promise to cover you as well as myself. If I tell you everything, then I shall be vouching for you, too. Staking my reputation on you. Maybe my life."

She opened her eyes wide to stare at him in wonder and doubt, but she could find no hint of anything bogus in his face or his tone. It seemed people still existed who talked in those terms, quite without cant.

"Do you want to know on those conditions? Remember, I shall then be relying upon you absolutely."

"You can," she said. "I won't breathe a word to any-one, I promise. Yes, I want to know."

"And you understand that it's a matter of national security that what I tell you should go no further?"

"Yes, I understand. You have my word." Her face was earnest with the terrible solemnity of youth. Yes, he thought, she had the generosity and imagination even to be able to keep secrets. And he stopped being afraid of her, just when he should have begun to be afraid.

He sat down with her on the antique bench in Chloe's

hall, and told her the whole story, suppressing nothing, not even the significance of the notebooks Alda had smuggled out of the country with him when he vanished.

For a moment, at the end of it, her sceptical mind revolted. Spies, counter-spies, defecting scientists, all exist, of course, but as sordid professionals fumbling grimy secrets of dubious value, for which governments must be crazy to pay out a farthing in bribes or wages. Not like this, not with ideals mixed up in the squalor, and patriotism—whatever that ought to mean, in these days of supranational aspirations—and honest, clean danger. It couldn't be true! Robert Welland was a romantic who had constructed a romantic's ingenious theory out of a few chance facts, and all he was going back to was the long, slow let-down into the untidy world of reality. He wouldn't find anything; there was nothing to find. Herbert Terrell had simply made a mis-step at last, the one that waits for every expert somewhere along the way, and fallen to his death.

Just for a moment she held the facts away from her, and saw them thus distantly and coolly; and then the whole erection of evidence toppled upon her and overwhelmed her, and she believed with all her heart, and was lost. She had no longer any defences against Terrell. He was dead, murdered, killed as the result of something he had undertaken out of his sense of duty to his profession and his country. He was more than she had ever given him a chance to show, and she owed him justice all the more now, because she had denied it to him living.

" So you see that everything possible will be done to find out the truth. And you will be very careful, won't you, not to let anything out even by accident? Remember I've vouched for you as for myself."

" I won't forget. I'm very grateful for your trust, I shan't betray it." She was staring before her with stunned eyes, seeing herself suddenly drawn, almost against her will, into a world of noble clichés, which she vehemently distrusted, but for which there existed no substitutes.

" And you'll try to set your mind at rest, and leave everything to us? I'm sorry that I've troubled your peace at all."

"Oh, no!" she said positively. "It's better to know." And to his question, with only the faintest note of reserve: "I know you'll do everything possible. And thank you!"

: :   : :

But he hadn't her personal obligations, and he hadn't her sense of guilt, and how could he expect her to sit back and let him lift the burden of her conscience and carry it away with him?

The first thing she looked round for, when he was gone, was the large-scale map of Central Europe she had just bought at Hatchards.

: :   : :

"Czech visas," said Toddy thoughtfully, "cost money." He sat back on his heels and pondered the delectable roads racing eastwards across the map, and his expression was speculative and tempted. "Not that I'm saying it wouldn't be a nice thing to do, mind you." He added ruefully: "Rather a lot of money, if you ask me!"

"I know they do, but look at the tourist exchange rate! We should more than get it back. And if we did decide on it, we could be through France and Germany in a couple of days. Eating in France is damned dear unless you picnic all the time, and who wants to do that? I bet we'd save by running through as quickly as possible, and surely Czechoslovakia would be a whole lot more interesting."

"I always did think you had a secret urge to live dangerously." Christine swung her legs from the edge of the table, and drew the crumbling Iron Curtain thoughtfully back into position with one toe. "Quite apart from prison cells, secret police, and all that guff—supposing it is guff, we could be wrong about that, too!—who does the talking?"

"We all do, in English. I'm told the Czechs are marvellous linguists, now's their chance to prove it. And if we do get out of bounds for English, I bet Toddy's German would get us by well enough." Tossa withdrew a little, to leave them with an idea they would soon be able to persuade themselves was their own. "Whatever you think, though,

I'm easy. But I'll write for visa applications if you like. They say it only takes a few days. I'm going to make some coffee," said Tossa, judging her moment nicely, and left them holding it.

" Maybe it does seem a pity not to use the carnet, now we've got it," said Christine reflectively.

" Quickest route on the map," reported Toddy, sprawled largely across Europe, " is Cassel—Brussels—Aachen, and straight down the autobahn. It takes you right past Wurzburg now, and part-way to Nuremberg. Might have got a bit farther, too, since this was printed."

" It's faster travelling through France than Belgium," warned Christine. " We could just as easily run through to Saarbrücken, and get on to the southern branch of the autobahn, and then go north to Frankfurt."

" It's miles longer."

" Yes, but hours faster."

Dominic, who had never yet driven on the Continent, said nothing, but sat back and let them argue it out. So it happened that he was the only one who did not miss the look on Tossa's face when she re-entered the room with the coffee tray, to find the twins deep in discussion of the various ways of reaching the Czech border quickly, and the possibilities presented once they had crossed it. He saw the small, fevered spark that lit in her eyes, the brief vindicated smile that touched the corners of her mouth, and ebbed again even more rapidly, leaving her fixed and sombre.

Tossa had what she wanted. But what it gave her was not pleasure, it seemed to him, only a brief and perilous sense of accomplishment, as if she had just taken the first step on a very uncertain journey.

Chapter 3

THE MAN WHO THUMBED A LIFT

They came spiralling down over France at about nine
o'clock on a fine Thursday morning, craning to see the
bewildering expanses of the blown sand-dunes revolve below
them, starred with little salt pools and furry with pines. The
estuary of the Canche dipped under one wing and vanished,
the bridge and its crawling beetles of cars disappeared. By
dazzling glimpses the white, urbane, anglicised villas winked
at them from among the trees, and the long beach trailed a
golden ribbon along the lacy edge of the sea. Le Touquet
would never be so beautiful again.

Twenty-five minutes after they had left England they
were creeping gingerly round the snack-bar called " L'Au-
bette," and into the groves of pines, round whose braced
feet the waves of sand broke like a patient and treacherous
sea. The first gendarme eyed them warily as they rolled
decorously round his concrete bollard, and bore away towards the golf links. Left turn after left turn, until you
cross the bridge over the Canche, and then sharp right.
And you've started. You're heading for Montreuil-sur-Mer
and the main Paris road; for Brussels and Aachen and the
Cologne-Frankfurt autobahn, and all points east.

" We're in France!" said Dominic, shattered and trans-
ported, for the first time relaxing the grim concentration
with which he was keeping to the right. " We're abroad!"

::   ::

They ran off the autobahn for their first night at the rest-
house at Siegburg, and thwarted of a bed there—it seemed
one must stop at about four o'clock to be sure of a room
anywhere immediately on the motorway—cruised down the
hill into the town, under the Michaelburg, and fetched up
in an embarrassingly narrow and difficult yard off the glit-

45

tering main street. Toddy parked the van gingerly in a cramped corner, and hugged himself at the thought of Dominic manipulating it out into traffic next morning. Every man for himself!

They strolled through the surprising glitter of the streets, still lively at past eight in the evening, and climbed the Michaelburg in the dusk to the fortress church.

And out of the blue Tossa made her next move.

"Wouldn't it be fine to go all the way east into Slovakia?" she said suddenly and fondly, as they sauntered down again through the silent gardens. "As far as the Tatras, anyhow. We *couldn't* go back without seeing the mountains."

"If we have time," agreed Toddy accommodatingly, willing to entertain all suggestions. "We've got to see Prague first."

The twins had known her for years, perhaps that was why their thumbs didn't prick. They knew her so well they'd stopped being sufficiently aware of her to question her attitudes and motives. What she offered, they accepted at its face value. Dominic had no such insulation. He walked beside her in the deepening dusk, her long, impetuous step almost a match for his, and felt some inexplicable tension drawing her taut as a bow-string.

It was at that moment that Dominic grasped, without any adequate grounds for his certainty, that she was steering this expedition carefully and patiently towards some end of her own. Hadn't she been the one who had suggested providing the car with a carnet? Wasn't it she who had thought of the Czech visas? Now, if he was right, she was making the next move, prodding them to hurry on eastwards into the Tatras; and *if* he was right, she would gently but doggedly persist until she got her own way.

"Why don't we just steam ahead right to the mountains," said Tossa, in the same brightly eager voice, "and take it easy on the way back? I've been had too many times, with the days running out because some gourmand for Gothic couldn't be dragged away from some cathedral or other. Make sure of the remotest bits first, *I* say. We know we've got to get back, let's make a point of getting *there*."

:   :   :   :

" Toddy! "

" Hallo? " mumbled Toddy sleepily, across the bedroom window silvered down one edge with moonlight. " What's up? "

" You know you told me Tossa's stepfather got killed, climbing somewhere? "

" Hmm, yes, what about him? "

" Was she fond of him at all? "

A snort of laughter from the other bed fetched an answering creak out of the pale, scrubbed wood of the bedstead. " Are you kidding? She couldn't stand him. He was so correct he made her want to throw things. Tossa left home, didn't even see much of her mother until she left this fellow for good. Why, what about him? "

" Oh, nothing. Just wondering if she had him on her mind, or something."

" Tossa misses him like you'd miss a rotten tooth. No, that's a lie, too, because since her mother left him she hasn't even felt any twinges. Even before he kicked off, he just wasn't there any more." A rustle of bedclothes and a lift in the sleepy voice indicated a quickening interest on Toddy's part : " Hey, Dom, you getting to like our Tossa? "

" She's all right," said Dominic sedately. " Bit prickly sometimes. Tod, where did this fellow kick off? "

" Oh, abroad, somewhere. Austria or Switzerland, or somewhere. Didn't check, actually. Does it matter? "

" Not a lot, I suppose. If you're dead you're dead. Good night, Tod! "

" Good night, Dom! That's final notice! "

" OK! Pass out, I've finished."

Toddy passed out with the aplomb of an exhausted child. They had had to rise in the middle of the night to drive down to the airport. Dominic, however, lay awake and alert. Toddy might not know where this chap Terrell had got himself killed, but according to Dominic's pricking thumbs Tossa knew. Tossa knew, and stage by stage she was taking them there, to the very region, to the very spot. What did she know of the Tatras, unless that Terrell had dived to his death somewhere round their granite planes? Why mention them, unless of fixed intent?

Dominic's father was a C.I.D. Detective-Inspector in a county force on the Welsh borders. Maybe there's something to police parentage that sets you nosing for mysteries wherever you go. Or maybe there was really something about Tossa's shuddering anticipation that justifiably set his flesh crawling. Whichever it was, Dominic was a long time falling asleep.

::   ::

They camped the next night, a little way short of the Czech border, in the beautiful, rolling, forest-and-meadow land of the Palatinate. And in the morning they crossed the frontier.

Waidhaus was quiet, efficient and polite, the Customs house poised on the edge of a sharp dip. Beyond the barrier the road curved away into Czechoslovakia, straightened again, and immediately began to climb; and there before them, on either side of the way, were the white buildings of the Czech Customs offices; and drawn up in the roadway on the near side of the barriers were at least a dozen cars, buses and caravans, from which at least fifty people had spilled out to flourish carnets and passports at harassed but amiable Czech officials.

It took them an hour to get through. There were more papers to be dealt with here, passports and visas, the carnet, the insurance document, as well as a polite and good-humoured pretence at examining their baggage, and a genuine scrutiny of the car.

" For the first time," said Christine approvingly, " I feel as if someone cares whether we've arrived or not. It got almost insulting, being waved from one country into another like tossing the morning paper over the gate."

" Not so cynical as the French," Toddy allowed judicially,

in an undertone, distributing their cleared passports. " Not so disdainfully efficient as the Germans. I like to see officials who sweat over the job, and aren't past getting excited. That immigration chap took a liking to your passport photograph, Tossa—even showed it to his mate at the other table. Come to look at it," he admitted, studying it impartially, " it isn't at all bad."

" Thank you !" said the saturnine young Czech who had been feigning to examine Tossa's suitcase, without so much as disarranging the one tissue-wrapped party dress she had popped in at the last moment " in case." " Everything is in order. You can proceed."

They piled eagerly into the van again, Dominic at the wheel. The Customs man signalled to the young soldier who held the chain of the barrier, and up went the pole. Gravely they acknowledged the salutes that ushered them through into a new country, and wormed their way through the congestion of cars and under the quivering pole.

" We're in !" breathed Christine, staggered to find it so easy.

" No iron curtain, no nothing," agreed Toddy, astonished in his turn. " A bit like crashing the sound barrier, though."

The van climbed out of the frontier hollow, between slopes of silver birches, under the distant shadow of the first of many castles, a gaunt ruin on a lush, wooded hill. They were surging merrily into full speed, when a second barrier loomed in sight, barring their road, and a tall wooden watch-tower beside it. The very young soldier on guard there glared with a solemnity beyond his seventeen years, as Dominic slowed to a discreet halt before the bar, and waited dutifully to see what was required of him.

With unshaken gravity the boy lifted a telephone from its stand in the box beside him, and consulted some unknown authority.

" No iron curtain?" whispered Christine, between apprehension and the giggles.

" Shut up, idiot !" hissed Toddy. " He's only doing his job."

The boy replaced the telephone with deliberation, walked round them, eyeing the girls with a curiosity that brought the transaction down to a completely human level, and hoisted the pole, motioning them through with only the most austere inclination of his head. He was very young, and took his duties seriously.

They saluted this gateman, too, but apart from a quickening spark in his eye he preserved his motionless dignity. Possibly he treasured the girls, acknowledging his services decorously from the rear windows; but if he did, he wasn't admitting it. Only when they were well away from him, soaring up the slope, did he suddenly lift one arm above his head, in a wave as impersonal as the hills.

They never even saw it; all their attention was fixed eagerly ahead, as Dominic accelerated happily towards the crest of the rise, among the shimmering birch trees.

A man's figure rose suddenly and joyously out of the ditch beside the road, and stood on the verge, energetically thumbing them to a standstill. A young, round, glowing face under a sunburst of blond hair beamed at them confidently, and had no doubts whatever of its warm and friendly welcome. A small rucksack swung from the cajoling arm that flagged them down. In the other hand he held a large open sandwich, which he balanced expertly as he ran alongside them and signalled, from ingenuous blue eyes and beaming mouth, his pleasure in having hooked so interesting, so rewarding a ride. The GB plate, the number, the girls, one glance and he had them all weighed up.

Dominic wound the window right down, and said: "Hallo!" As an obvious greeting he didn't see why it shouldn't do just as well as any other; but in spite of Tossa's predictions he was hardly prepared to be addressed promptly and fluently in his own language.

"Good morning!" said the beaming young man, tilting his open sandwich just in time to retrieve a slipping gherkin. "Please excuse that I trouble you, but if you go to Prague, may I ride with you? If you have room?" He knew they had room, he had practically measured their cubic content with that one expert flick of a blond eyelash. " I could be of help, if you do not know the road. To work my passage, I shall be the guide, if you permit?"

Toddy not only permitted; he applauded. He enjoyed driving, but to him navigating was a chore. He cast a glance behind him at the empty road, and was out of the front passenger seat like a greyhound from its trap.

" It's all yours! Here, give me your rucksack, I'll stow it in the back with our stuff, and you take this seat."

" But you are sure? The ladies will not mind if I ride with you? I should not like to be a burden, and some people do not approve of auto-stop."

They assured him that this method of travelling was well-established even in England, and that they had no personal objection to it, had even used it on occasions. They installed the young man, his sandwich, and his rucksack. Christine, rendered thoughtful by the last glimpse of the gherkin as it vanished behind strong white teeth, reached into the food-box and began to compile a mid-morning snack.

" You are also students?" asked their new passenger, as they drove through Rozvadov, a nondescript street-village hardly different from those they had left on the other side of the frontier, except that, lacking the exact German tidiness, it appeared a little shaggier and dustier. " My name is Miroslav Zachar. To my friends Mirek—you will find it easier to remember. I am student of philosophy."

They told him freely who they were, and what they were reading, and he overflowed with uninhibited questions, produced so naturally and confidently that it was impossible to find any of them offensive. They were on vacation, of course, like him? Was it their first visit to Czechoslovakia? Where were they going to stay in Prague? And where else did they intend to go? He was full of helpful suggestions. Castles, lakes, towns, he knew them all.

" You must do quite a lot of auto-stopping," said Christine, busy with cheese and crackers. " You seem to have been everywhere."

" I do it a lot, yes. Every holiday. Sometimes I go with

friends, sometimes alone. It is better alone. For one
person it is easy to get a lift."

"And what made you come all the way out here? You
do live in Prague?"

"I have been walking in these hills of the Bohemian
Forest. Now I come back to the road, hoping to get a lift
back into Prague quickly. This is a good place, foreign
cars coming in here, naturally they rush straight to Prague.
But I am lucky to meet some more students. That's nice!
I'm glad I time it so good. No, in Prague I have an uncle
and aunt, if you will kindly take me so far I can stay with
them, and afterwards stop another car," he said serenely,
"to take me on eastwards. Because of course you will be
staying in Prague."

"Perhaps only for one or two nights," Tossa said suddenly, in that gruff boyish croak of hers, that could be so
disconcerting to the unaccustomed ear.

They were on a stretch of road complicated by many
climbing bends among trees, but without forks where
Dominic could possibly go wrong. Miroslav Zachar abandoned his navigating for a moment to turn his head and
study this dark-brown girl seriously. His amiable moon-face
shone upon her approvingly.

"You will be going on so soon? But where?"

"Into Slovakia," she said quite positively, asking no
one's agreement.

"No, really? You go to Bratislava, perhaps?"

"No," she said, with the same authority; and if no one
took her up on it now they were quite certainly committed.
And no one did. "No, we want to go to the Tatras. We
can make a longer stay in Prague on the way back. Is that
the same way you wanted to go? You did say eastwards.
Where is your home?"

"My home," said Mirek, delighted, "is in Liptovsky
Mikuláš. That is very near the Tatra range. If you are
really going so far, and if you would like to have a guide,
believe me, I will make it easy for you, I will take care of
everything. You have rooms in Prague? No? I can ar-

range it. The Students' Union will manage it for us, you'll see. And I will show you the city. I know it like my hand. How long you would like to stay? One night? Two nights? I shall make a programme for you. And then you will take me with you to Slovakia? I know the best camping-ground on the way, in Javorník, in the most beautiful hills. Oh, I shall work my passage, you will see!"

It sounded like the answer to everything. The others might have demurred at leaving Prague so soon in other circumstances, but with a heaven-sent guide added to the party, gratis, it seemed much the most practical and economic solution to run right through, as Tossa had urged, spend as long as possible in the east, and then make their way back, without a guide, over a road already travelled once. Even if they saw fit to vary it, they would at least know the lie of the land.

"It's a bargain!" said Tossa, incandescent with eagerness. "One night in Prague, if you can really work it for us. . . ."

"Two!" Christine demurred.

"One! We shall come back, and we shall know the basic lay-out then, we can easily find our way around. And then we go on to the Tatras. Mirek, you must know those parts awfully well, if it's your home. Do you know a place —not in the High Tatras, actually, in the Low Tatras— called Zbojská Dolina?"

"Dig that!" said Toddy, impressed. "The girl's been studying the map."

"You have so good a map?" Mirek was astonished and respectful. "It is only a small valley. I think it is not marked on any map I know. We do not have many such large-scale maps for walking, like yours."

Tossa fortified herself with a large bite from her cheese cracker, and made the most of the muffling noise. "No, it isn't on the maps. I knew somebody once who stayed there, and they—she—said it was lovely. I always thought I'd like to go there."

Geese, parading the dusty open green of the small town

of Bor, scuffled with indignant shrieks from before the
wheels of the van. The small, dilapidated castle mouldered
peacefully among its trees on their right, as they curled
through the single deserted street. Everything was coloured
a faint, neutral brown. New pastel paint would have
shattered a sacred silence. Border Bohemia drowsed, veiled
itself, and let them pass by.

"Hey!" reminded Dominic peremptorily. "Which way
at this fork? I can't see any 'Praha'."

Children at the crossroads, in diminutive shorts and faded
cotton sweaters, bounced, smiled and waved at them energetically. Of the welcome extended to foreigners, on this
level, there was no possible doubt. They were the glitter in
the children's world.

"To the left," said Mirek, sliding hastily back to his
duty.

"This friend of mine," Tossa's voice persisted, doggedly
offhand behind Dominic's shoulders, "stayed at a little inn
somewhere in this Zbojská Dolina. It was called the Riavka
hut. Do you know it?"

They cruised down into a river valley, level green
meadows on the near side of it, a sharp escarpment beyond,
and climbed out again by a winding road, glimpsing silver
on either hand as they turned.

"Why, yes, surely I know it," said Mirek.

"My friend said it was lovely walking country there. We
like to walk. Do you think we could get rooms at this
Riavka hut? Do you think the Students' Union would try
to arrange it for us?"

They were climbing steadily into the little town of
Stríbro.

"It means silver," explained Mirek, as they wound their
way into the square, and turned sharp right out of it, to un-
coil in a long spiral down the mount on which the town was
built. "Here there were silver mines." And to Tossa, without turning his head, he said cheerfully: "Yes, they can
arrange it. I shall do it for you. For you I shall do everything you wish."

And not one of them had questioned this sudden detailed knowledge she had displayed of the region to which they were bound; no one had marvelled, and it was too late to marvel now. She had the whole expedition in her hands. They were going where, for her own inscrutable purpose, Tossa wished to go.

::   ::

Mirek showed them Prague. Seeing they had tamely submitted to staying only one night in that delectable city, it was amazing how much he did manage to show them. The shopping centre, based firmly upon the great, broad thoroughfare of Wenceslas Square and the two streets forking from its massive foot, was concentrated enough to be viewed quite easily and quickly. But how did he manage to get them to Hradcany, that magical castle-quarter walled like a town within the fortress ramparts high above the Vltava river, and also out to the Mozart Museum in its lost, enchanted garden south of the town? It was impossible in the time, but Mirek did it. He showed them the little monastery of Loretto, long monkless, with its honeyed carillon of bells and its blinding treasury. He showed them the eleventh-century hall deep beneath the castle, austere, imaginatively restored and imperishably beautiful, after which all the loftier and later layers were anticlimax. And late in the evening he showed them a very handsome dinner, and two tiny night-clubs, each with an incomprehensible but apparently sophisticated cabaret.

They fell asleep in the beds Mirek had found for them, with a picture of Prague behind their eyelids, shabby, neutral-tinted, mouldering, gracious, imperial, drab, flamboyant, invulnerably beautiful; so old that it was indifferent to criticism; so assured that it turned a deaf ear to praise. The dirty industrial quarters hanging on its skirts were merely the soiled ruffles of an empress, dulled by one day's wear. The fall of the tumbling terraced gardens beneath the castle, encrusted with stone statuary and grottoes and galleries, was a cascade of lace on the imperial bosom, heady and fresh as the acacia sweetness that hung on the night air.

And the next day they headed eastward for Slovakia.

:   :   :   :

They drove down out of the Javorník hills at leisure from their night camp, and into the town of Zilina. Beyond the civic buildings in the town square the crests of farther hills hung in the sky, pointed, shaggy, forested, the cones and pyramids of the Little Fatras. Mirek, moved to ecstasies of local patriotism as soon as he stood on Slovak soil, had whiled away the miles by telling them the story of Janosík, the Slovak outlaw-hero, who took to the hills here with his eleven mountain boys, in revolt against the feudal tyranny that kept his countrymen serfs. Born in the Fatra Hills, he died at last on a gallows at Liptovsky Mikulás, and after him all the mountain boys died tragic deaths. No happy ending for them; the usual comparison with Robin Hood, said Mirek a little didactically, foundered on that rock of martyrdom. There were many songs about Janosík, and Mirek knew them all. It took the waft of coffee from the foyer of the hotel to silence him.

" You'd like the second breakfast here? We're not in a hurry to-day, and the next stretch is wonderful. You will want to stop and take pictures."

They agreed that they could do with coffee. Toddy turned the van from the road, and let it run gently into the parking-ground along the hotel frontage.

" Look! An MG!" Christine halted them delightedly to admire a car from home. " No GB. Diplomatic plates! Somebody from the embassy must be here."

" Idiot!" said Toddy amiably. " It doesn't have to be an English owner. Probably United Arab Republic, or something. Half the world buys British when it comes to cars, especially semi-sports jobs like this."

" There's a suitcase on the back seat, anyhow." Christine had already caught the Czech habit of walking all round unfamiliar cars and examining them closely, without the least embarrassment or offence. " So he's not staying here, only halting like us. Maybe he smelled the coffee, too.

What'll you bet I can't pick him out in the kavárna?" She had adopted the Czech word for café, it came more naturally now than the French; and since in English both were borrowed, why not use the native one?

" If you know the code," said Toddy, " you can tell by the registration letters which embassy it belongs to. Do you know, Mirek?"

" It is someone from the British Embassy," said Mirek at once.

Tossa's warm, rose-olive complexion protected her from betrayal by pallor or blushing, and her silences were quite inscrutable. She looked the MG over, and dismissed it from her notice. " Come on," she said impatiently, " I'm famished for that coffee." And she led the way in through the cool, dim foyer, shoving the kavárna door open with a heave of her shoulder, and marching across the room to appropriate a table by the window.

" Mostly Czechs," reported Christine confidently, looking round with interest as she sat down at the marble-topped table, scaled to allow half a dozen people to spread their elbows comfortably.

A white-aproned waiter came bustling to take their order. They left the talking to Mirek. Their only complaint against him was that he made everything too easy; but the time was coming when he would leave them to their own limited resources.

" Got him!" Christine proclaimed with satisfaction. " Don't look round yet, he's looking this way. In the corner away to the left, close to the mirror. Wait a moment, I'll tell you when you can look. But that's him! He couldn't be anything but English. Mirek, do *we* go around looking as conspicuous as *that*?"

" Hurry up!" protested Toddy. " I'm getting a stiff neck, trying not to turn round. Can I look yet?"

" Not yet. I'll tell you when. *Now, quick!* He's just talking to the waiter."

She was right, of course. There was only one person there

who had to be English. You could almost say he had to be
an English diplomat. Quite young, about thirty, dressed for
the country, but so correctly that he retained a look of the
town. Nondescriptly fair, rather lightly-boned among these
solid square Czechs and gaunt, rakish Slovaks, withdrawn,
gentle, formal. The cut of his sportscoat gave him away,
and the Paisley silk scarf knotted in the throat of his open
shirt. Even the way he drank his coffee was unmistakably
English.

"Funny!" sighed Toddy. "You never notice anything
special about people when they're at home. Man, does it
stick out here!" He plumped his chin into a resigned palm,
groaning. "I give up! I bet from over there I look just like
that!"

"Oh, not quite," said Mirek comfortingly. "One could
say, perhaps, English on sight, but not *embassy* English.
More student English. It is a distinction."

"Thank you! Thank you very much! I don't *want* to
be identifiable at a hundred yards."

"Why not?" said Mirek disarmingly. "Are you ashamed
of it?"

"He looks lonely," said Christine. "Shouldn't we pick
him up? It would be quite easy. He's giving Tossa the eye,
anyhow."

Tossa turned and gave the distant customer a long, considering look. Not a muscle of her smooth oval face
quivered. "Not my type," she said, after a merciless
scrutiny, and turned back to her coffee. "Anyhow, he's
probably heading the other way, back to Prague."

Christine shut her eyes for a moment to reckon up the
days since they had left England. "Monday! Yes, I suppose he could be. Back to the grindstone after a week-end
in Slovakia. But the way the car's parked, I'd have
thought he was going our way."

Dominic had been thinking the very same thing, and was
thinking it still; and the thought had first entered his mind
in the instant when Tossa's eyes had encountered those of
the Englishman in the distant corner, held his gaze just long

enough to register detached and unrecognising curiosity, and moved on just in time to avoid any suggestion of rudeness. For the man hadn't been quite so adroit. He hadn't the kind of face that gives much away, but for one instant there had been a kindling of his eyes, a sharpening of his attention, the unmistakable, instantaneous light of recognition. It was gone in an instant, too, without trace. He looked at her now with interest and approval across the room but as if he had never seen her in his life before.

Because he had recovered himself, and suppressed what she must not be allowed to see? Or because he had taken a hint from her cool, impersonal glance, and responded in kind as soon as he had grasped what she wanted? If the second, then they were in this curious affair together, and yet separately, for plainly he hadn't expected Tossa to show up here in the middle of Europe, but equally plainly he had hastened to conform to what she desired when she did inexplicably appear. And if the first? Then Tossa wasn't acting; he knew her but she did not know him, and there was something in the air important enough—or sinister enough—to make it expedient for him to dissemble his knowledge.

Dominic drank his coffee, and let their chatter ricochet round him; he was beginning not to like this secrecy at all. Tossa's affairs were her own, but after all, here they were seven hundred miles or more from home, in an alien, and some would even have said an enemy, country. There had been one death, a death which began now to look more and more suspect. Beyond question Tossa was up to something, biting off, perhaps, much more than she could chew. And what could he do? Nothing, not even question her or offer help, unless she showed a disposition to want it, and that was the last thing he expected from Tossa. Nothing in the world he could do, except, perhaps, stay close to her and keep his eyes open.

When they paid for their coffee and left, Tossa walked out without so much as a glance in the stranger's direction; but Dominic, looking back quickly from the doorway, saw that the waiter was just threading his way between the tables towards the Englishman's corner.

In the foyer Tossa halted, rummaging like a terrier in the depths of her overcrowded handbag after powder and comb. "You go ahead, I'll be with you in a minute." She wandered off questingly towards the back of the hall, and left them to make their way out into the sunshine without her.

Dominic let the others go on ahead, and halted on the pavement a step aside from the doorway. The wide glass door was fastened fully open, and the dimness of the wall behind turned it into a very passable mirror. It showed him, darkly but distinctly, a segment of the foyer which included the door of the kavárna, just swinging back after the passage of a waiter with a tray of beer-tankards. A moment more, and the door swung again, more sedately, and the solitary young man came out into the hall, looked round him quickly, and began to read the cinema posters on the baize notice-board.

The clack of Tossa's sandals echoed lightly from the rear corridors, and she came into sight, first a pale shadow in the glass, then rapidly growing clearer and closer. She passed by the young man without a glance, busily stuffing her powder compact back into her bag. Something oblong and small dropped out of the bulging outer pocket just before she snapped the catch.

Dominic ought, of course, to have turned in at the doorway to meet her, and called her attention at once to whatever it was she had let fall. Instead, he leaped away from the wall like a scalded cat, and by the time she emerged he was strolling round the corner after the others, looking back at the turn for her, and waiting to be overtaken. She came up with him brisk and smiling, and even slipped her hand in his arm as they fell into step together, a thing she had never done before.

He had hardly understood what he himself had just done, and why, until he felt her fingers close warmly on his sleeve, and realised with a startling surge of bitterness that even that touch was merely a part of her camouflage. It wasn't that he blamed her for making use of whatever came to hand, if she had such an urgent need to cover her secret; but he did resent being made the recipient of a first small mark of intimacy for so humiliating a reason. It hadn't dawned on him until then that she might be going to matter very much indeed in his life. And this, he thought bitterly, counting the seconds before the MG man should come hurrying after them, is a fine time to realise it!

Toddy and Christine had the map spread out against the side of the van, and were tracing the next stage of the drive.

"We are about to enter," proclaimed Toddy, turning from his explorations to report to the late-comers, "the spectacular gorge of the Váh, clean through the Little Fatras, passing close by the romantic ruins of Strecno castle and Stary Hrad—to name but a few! Come on, pile in. I'm driving."

The young man from the MG came bustling round the corner at that moment, and seeing them already embarking, broke into a light run, and waved an arresting arm.

"Excuse me! Just a moment!"

Nearly two minutes, thought Dominic. Time to read a few words, or write a few words, or both. Provided she passed him something a message could be hidden in properly.

She had. What the young man held out, as he came up panting and smiling, was her little leather comb-case, an ideal receptacle for a folded slip of paper.

"Excuse me, I was in the hall just now, I believe you dropped this as you were leaving."

She took it, astonished and charmingly vexed at her own carelessness, and voluble in thanks to him.

"Not at all! I'm glad I caught you in time." He withdrew a step or two, making it clear he had no wish to detain them. "You're on holiday?" He looked round them all, memorising faces, his smile a shade too bright, but then, he had every mark of a naturally shy and serious young man. "You're going on into the mountains?"

They made dutiful conversation, as one does when the encounter can be only a couple of minutes long, and probably will never be repeated. There is an art in touching deftly and graciously, and leaving a pleasant warmth behind on such occasions. On the whole, the young do it better than anyone.

"I'm sure you'll like it in Slovakia. There's lovely country to be explored here. Well, *bon voyage*! Have a good time!"

He drew back a few more steps, and then wheeled and walked smartly away from them. Tossa, with admirable calm, shoved the comb-case into her bag without a glance, and climbed into the van.

And no one else, thought Dominic, handing Christine in after her, had noticed a thing amiss with that little scene. Or could he really be sure of that? The twins would have given tongue at once, almost certainly. But who could be sure how much this pleasant fellow Miroslav noticed, or how deep he was? Or, for that matter, he thought for the first time, and with a sudden sickening lurch of his heart, who or what he was?

"Didn't play that one very well," said Christine critically, as they took the road eastwards out of Zilina. "After hooking him so neatly, too."

"Too little!" responded Tossa automatically. "I threw him back. Anyhow," she added wickedly, with a smile of pure defiance, "I got my bait back, didn't I?"

    : :   : :

The oddest thing in their three-day acquaintance with Mirek happened when he took his leave of them. And of all people, it was Tossa who precipitated it.

He brought them safely to Zbojská Dolina by mid-afternoon, himself driving the van up the last two miles of rough and narrow mountain track to the Riavka hut, and there confiding them to the care of the Martínek family. He fulfilled, in fact, everything he had undertaken for them, and everything he had claimed for himself was proved true. Clearly he was indeed a local man, well known here, for Martínek senior hailed him from the open cellar-flap of the inn with a welcoming roar as soon as he blew the horn at the log gate, and Martínek junior, higher up the incredibly green valley pastures with two rangy dogs, whistled and waved. Mrs. Martínek came hurrying out from the kitchen to the bar, the scrubbed boards creaking to her quick steps, and shook Mirek by the hand warmly but casually, as a crony's son from the next village rather than a rare and honoured visitor. Any friend of Mirek's, clearly, was welcome here.

All the doubts and suspicions that had been haunting Dominic's mind since morning were blown away. He felt ashamed and confounded. There were, it seemed, still people in the world who had nothing to hide, and were exactly what they purported to be.

" I leave you now," announced Mirek, beaming at them over the pile of luggage he had assembled on the bar floor. "You will be all right with Mrs. Martínek, she has two rooms for you, and everything is prepared. You can talk to her in German, she understands it a little. And Dana— she speaks English, enough for every day. So now I shall go home. I thank you very much for such a pleasant ride, and I hope we shall meet again some day."

It was an honest farewell speech if ever they'd heard one. He shook hands all round, his rucksack already hoisted on his shoulder.

"But how far have you to go?" Toddy demanded. "After all you've done for us, you must let us drive you home. Or at least down to the road. Oh, nonsense, you must! We know this road now, we're home and dry, now let's see you home."

But Mirek wouldn't hear of it. He laughed the offer out of the bar window. "All this time I have no exercise, these few miles to my home I must walk. Often I walk the length of Slovakia on vacation. No, no, no, you will have your own walking to do." He held out his hand to Christine. "I have been very happy, getting to know you all. It was for me a great pleasure."

When he reached Tossa, she was gazing up into his face with the most curious expression, half sullen and half guilty; and Dominic saw with astonishment that there were tears in her eyes. As they shook hands she suddenly reached up on tip-toe, and kissed Mirek's round brick-red cheek very quickly and awkwardly.

"Mirek," she said impulsively, "you've been absolutely everything some people at home would like to think Czech people *aren't*—so kind, and warm, and *sincere*. I can't tell you how much I've appreciated it."

This extrovert behaviour was staggering enough in their moody, insecure and sceptical Tossa; but before they had time to wonder at it, something even more surprising had manifested itself in Mirek. Out of the collar of his open-necked shirt surged like a tide the most stupendous blush they had ever seen, engulfing muscular neck and tanned cheeks, burning in the lobes of his ears, and washing triumphantly into the roots of his blond hair. He stood looking down at Tossa from behind this crimson cloud, his pleasant features fixed in mid-smile, and his blue eyes helpless and horrified. He couldn't even think of a joke to turn the moment aside, it was Toddy who had to prick the bubble of constraint and set him free to go.

"You know what the English are," said Toddy indulgently, "well-meaning but imprecise. The girl means *Slovak* people, of course!"

Chapter 4

THE MAN WHO KEPT THE SCORE

The Riavka hut took its name from the brook that came bounding down Zbojská Dolina from its source in the topmost bowl of the valley, "riavka" being a Slovak diminutive for just such an upland river. It looked very much like any other mountain hut in any other high range anywhere in Europe, a large, rambling, two-storied house, part stone, part wood, with heavily overhanging eaves, railed verandas, and firewood and logs stacked neatly beneath the overhang all along one wall. Besides being an inn for the herdsmen and the occasional rambler, it was also a farm and a timber-station, and a whole conglomeration of low wooden buildings clung to the outer log fence that bounded its garden and paddock. It stood in lush green meadows, a third of the way up the valley, and cows and horses grazed freely to the edge of the conifer belt that engulfed the path a few hundred yards above the house.

Beyond was deep forest, the brook purling and rippling away busily somewhere on their left hand, until they crossed it by a log bridge, and walked for some way on a rock causeway poised high above it. The pines and firs absorbed the heat of the sun, and transmitted it to earth as a heavy, intoxicating scent as thick as resin. The padding of needles under their feet was deep and spongy, and there were huge boletus mushrooms bursting through it here and there, and colonies of slim yellow "foxes" like pale fingers parting the mould. In the more open places, where the heat of the sun poured through upon them suddenly like laughter, and the ripe August grass grew waist-high, the air was rich with a spicy sweetness that would always thereafter mean hot summer woods to them, the scent of raspberries. The wild canes grew in thick clumps among the grass, heavy

65

with fruit. They picked handfuls, and walked on, eating them.

Beyond the belt of woodland there were broken areas of outcrop rocks and boulders, the interstices of the rocks full of flowers, heaths and stonecrops and alpine roses. The path, partly natural, partly laid with flat stones, wound bewilderingly through this miniature rock town, taking the easiest way. They had lost the brook now, it ran somewhere in the deep cleft that fell away on their right; but beyond the point where the rocks gave place again to higher, drier meadows they kept company with it again for a while, and crossed it again. In the greener, moist patches here there were gentians of several tints and sizes, and the colours of quite ordinary flowers, as is their way in the mountains, had darkened into glowing brilliance, the scabious royal purple, the coltsfoot burning orange.

They were overshadowed now on either side by scree slopes and striated faces of rock. If a climber wanted a little practice in Zbojská Dolina, this was where he would have to come. There were a few nice rock pitches leaning over them here, a few limestone needles of the kind experts like to play with when the snow-peaks are out of reach. Ahead of them, on a low shelf on the right-hand side of the valley, and almost thrust from its precarious perch by boulders settling at the foot of the scree, sat a small white building, its squat walls leaning inward with a heavy batter, a tiny lantern tower crowning its roof. The door, as the sunlight showed them, leaned half-open, its upper hinge broken.

"Wonder what that is?" Christine said.

"It's a chapel," said Tossa. "Some people got snow-bound here once, and died of exposure, so they built a little refuge in case the same thing happened to somebody else. That sort of chapel, not one for holding services."

"How did you find all that out?" demanded Toddy. "It isn't in the guide-book."

"Dana told me. I was asking her about the valley just before we came out, that's all." Tossa took a wide, measuring look round her, at all the exposed faces of rock, and her gaze settled with a swoop upon the pallid scar of a path that crossed the mountainside on the opposite slope, on a level slightly higher than the roof of the chapel. Above the mark the oblique, striated rock rose steeply, below it was almost sheer for fifty feet or so. But for one excrescence where a harder stratum had refused to weather at the general speed, it would have been a perfectly straight line that crossed the cliff, from the crest on one side to a fold of bushes and trees on the other, descending perhaps fifteen feet in the process. But at the nose of harder limestone the path turned sharply, making a careful blind bend round the obstruction. The result looked, from here, like a large, bold tick slashed across a slate.

Tossa hitched her camera round her neck, and left the path. Without a word she turned towards that face of rock, studying it all the while with drawn brows and jutting lip as she went, and set a straight course for the foot of it across the strip of meadow and into the fringe of bushes.

They all followed her docilely. Dominic would have followed her in any case, and the twins didn't care which direction they took, where all was new and the sun was shining. Almost imperceptibly, for these very reasons, they had arrived at an arrangement by which Tossa constantly set the course, and the others fell into line after her; for Tossa did care where she went. Tossa was a woman with a purpose. Through the trees she led them, following her nose blindly now, or perhaps drawn by the invisible thread of tension that had compelled her across Europe. Her navigation was accurate enough. She came to the spot where the trees fell away, then to the first slanting tables of outcrop rock, tilted at the same angle as the strata in the exposed face above. The cliff hung like a pale grey curtain over them, the heat of the sun rebounding from it into their faces. A broad limestone shelf, moving upward in three irregular steps, jutted from the foot of the pleated folds.

" Where are we going?" asked Christine idly, not greatly concerned about the answer.

"Oh, we'll go on up the valley in a minute." Tossa

squinted experimentally and almost convincingly into the
view-finder, and backed a little from the cliff. " I just
thought this would make a fine backcloth for a picture."

If it was simply an excuse for her detour, it wasn't a bad
one. The light was fingering every pleat in the rock curtain
like the quivering strings of a harp, and she had space
enough to get plenty of contrast and scope into her picture.

"Would you mind disposing yourselves nicely on the
seats so thoughtfully provided for you? One on each step.
A little more to the left, please, Chris. *My* left, you nut!
Yes, that's fine! Hold it!"

They clambered obediently up the shelf of limestone, and
sat down where she directed, while she made two exposures,
and took her time about it. As she lowered the camera for
the second time, Dominic saw her raise her head and cast
one rapid glance at the cliff directly above the spot where
he was sitting; and because she had just uncovered her face
it was for once a naked and readable glance, fierce and
doubtful and afraid, and aching with a dark, suppressed
excitement that disquieted him horribly.

It was gone in a moment, she was winding her film on
and waving them down. The others had noticed nothing,
because they were looking for nothing. But Dominic cast
one quick glance upwards, where she had looked, and saw
that he had been sitting right beneath the jagged nose of
rock that jutted to form the angle of the path above.

He felt a light sweat break on his forehead and lip, as
understanding broke like a flush of sudden heat in his mind.
Tossa on a trail was single-minded to the point of ruthless-
ness. That projection of rock up there, making a blind cross
with the face of the cliff against the sky, was the cross that
marked the spot where the accident occurred. He was sitting in the very place where Tossa's stepfather had crashed
to his death.

: :   : :

Dana Martínek was alone in the bar when Dominic went
in to order their coffee that evening. He had hoped she
would be. His friends were sitting on the little front ter-

race under the stars, well out of earshot. If he was making a fool of himself, concocting a melodrama out of a few trivial incidents and Tossa's moodiness, now was the time to find out and alter course.

"Miss Martínek, we've been up as far as the chapel this afternoon. Just opposite there, on the other side of the brook, there's an almost sheer rock face, with a path crossing it. You know the place I mean?"

She turned from the washing of glasses to look at him curiously; a tall girl, not pretty, but with the composed and confident carriage which was common among young women here, and a cast of face to which he was becoming accustomed, wide-boned but softly and smoothly fleshed, widest across the eyes, which were themselves rounded and full and clear. Eyes that could conceal with perfect coolness; but what they did choose to confide, he thought, would be the truth.

"Yes, I know it," she said, volunteering nothing.

"Wasn't somebody killed in this valley only a couple of weeks or so ago? An Englishman who was staying here?"

She said: "Yes," without any particular reluctance or hesitation, but that was all.

"And was that the place where it happened? He fell from that path on to the rock?" His spine chilled at the thought that he had been sitting there, posing for a photograph. "Miss Martínek. . . ."

Burningly candid faces like hers could withhold smiles, too, their assurance made it possible to be grave even at close quarters and with strangers. But she smiled at him then, not without a touch of amusement in the goodwill. She was twenty-one, two good years older than Dominic.

"You may call me Dana, if you like. It is quicker. Yes, you are right, it was there that he fell."

"From that bend in the path?"

"So it seemed."

"Would you mind telling me about it?"

"What is there to tell? Mr. Terrell came here and wished to stay, and the room was free, because one couple who should have come had illness at home. So of course, we took him. He was out alone all day. That's normal for people who come here, at least when the weather is good. So we were not worried on the third evening, when he did not come back until dark. But by ten o'clock we grew anxious, and alerted the mountain patrol, and went out ourselves with lights, to search in the head of the valley. But we were not the first to find him. When we got there the police from Liptovsky Pavol were already there. He was dead when they found him."

"The police? But you hadn't notified the police, had you? Only the mountain rescue people."

She shrugged. "The patrol must have called the police, I suppose. They were there. It was they who found him."

"And his injuries? Did it seem as if they *were* the result of a fall like that?"

She looked him in the eye for a moment, very gravely. "Mr. Felse. . . ."

"You may call me Dominic," he said, with a grin that managed to be unwontedly impudent because of his nervousness. "It takes longer, but it's more friendly."

"Dominic," said Dana, her smile reappearing for a moment, "you should ask the police these questions. I did not have to go and look at that poor man broken on a slab of limestone, and so I did not go. All I know is what my father said, and he helped to carry him. You know what such a fall on such a surface could do to a man's bones, how many fractures there would be, what sort of fractures? Yes, he was like that. Yes, he fell. You do not get like he was in any other way. They say he died within a few minutes, maybe almost instantly. And I think you have too romantic an imagination, you should curb it."

"Not me," said Dominic, taking his elbows from the bar with a sigh. "It isn't that easy. Well, thanks, anyhow. I'll take the coffee out, shall I, and save you a journey."

While she was making it he thought of another question. "What sort of equipment was he carrying, this Mr. Terrell?"

He had hardly expected very much from that, but she turned and looked at him with interest. " Yes, that was perhaps odd. He had with him ice-axe, nylon ropes, *kletter-schuhe*, everything for climbing. Naturally he did not carry or need them here. But perhaps it is not so strange, because he came here from the High Tatras. You know them, the big mountains, you must have seen them across the valley as you came from Ruzomberok."

"Yes," he agreed eagerly, remembering how abruptly that sickle of icy heads had appeared in the sky on their left hand, like a mirage of snow-fields and honed blue slopes and trailing banners of cloud beyond the green, lush flats of the Váh, fifteen miles wide. " Yes, *there* he'd want his kit."

" I asked him how he could bear to leave Strbské Pleso, but he said he had pulled a muscle in his arm, so he, came away where he could walk, and not be tempted to use it too soon."

" Strbské Pleso? That's where he was staying, over there?"

" It means the lake of Strba. It is at the western end of the Freedom Road, that high-level road that runs along the range. Hand me that tray, will you, please? So, and there is your coffee."

He thanked her, and lifted the tray, balancing it carefully. He had reached the doorway, encrusted with stars, when she said quietly behind him : " Dominic. . . ."

" Yes?" He turned his head alertly.

" Do you know you have been asking me all the same questions your friend asked me this afternoon? The little dark girl—Miss Barber, I think she is called."

" Yes . . . I thought she might have," said Dominic, and wavered in the doorway for a moment more. " Did she ask what hotel he was staying at, over there?"

" No, she did not. But in any case he did not tell me that, and I did not ask him."

" All right. Thanks, anyhow!"

He carried the tray of coffee out to the terrace. It was not at all surprising that he should arrive just in time to hear

Tossa saying, with the sinister, bright edge to her voice that he was beginning to know only too well: "How about making a sortie over into the High Tatras, to-morrow?"

: :   : :

All the way along the winding road that brought them out of the range, with the enchanting little river bounding and sparkling on their left hand, and the firs standing ankle-deep in ferns along its rim, Dominic was waiting with nerves at stretch to see how she would manage to direct their movements exactly where she wanted to go, and how much she would give away in the process.

"To the right," Tossa instructed him, poring over the map as though she had not already learned it by heart, "and keep on the signs for Poprad."

At Liptovsky Hradok there was a promising fork, where the left-hand road seemed to set course directly for the roots of the mountains.

"Don't take it," warned Tossa, "keep on towards Poprad. It doesn't join the Freedom Road, it goes straight over into Poland, and we can't go, and anyhow I think the frontier's closed there. It's a broken line on this map. There's a left fork from this road, oh, twenty kilometres on, that takes us up on to this Freedom Road, and then it runs on along the range all the rest of the way."

All of which Dominic knew as well as she did; he'd been doing his homework even more industriously. He also knew that the first-class route up to the Freedom Road was nearer forty kilometres ahead than twenty, and joined the shelf highway in mid-course; but the turning to which she was directing them, short, second-class and quite certainly extremely steep to make the gradient in the distance, would lead them to the western end of the upper road, and straight to the lake of Strba.

That didn't take much accounting for, of course; so much she had learned from Dana. What he was waiting to see was what she would do and where she would lead them when they got there. Because she wouldn't know precisely where to look for her stepfather's traces in the lake resort, unless she had information Dana didn't possess.

The road streamed eastward along the floor of the great valley, threading the cobbled streets and spacious squares of small towns, and emerging again into the empty, verdant fields, that fantastic back-drop of peaks still unrolling steadily beside it.

Two main streams combine to form the river Váh, the White Váh the white mountain water from the High Tatras, the Black Váh from the district of Mount Royal in the Low Tatras. Their road crossed the White Váh for the last time, not many miles from its source, and they were over an imperceptible water-shed, no more than the heaving of a sigh from the valley's great green heart, that separated the westward-flowing Váh from the eastward-flowing tributaries of the Poprad, which is itself a tributary of the Dunajec, and joins it to wander away northward into Poland beyond the Tatra range. Those tiny streams they were leaving were the last of the Danube basin. This new and even tinier one, crossed soon after they turned on to Tossa's climbing road and headed precipitately towards the foothills, was the first innocent trickle of the vast drainage area of the Vistula. A couple of miles and a slight heave in the level of the plain determined their eternal separation.

The van climbed dizzily, on a roughly-surfaced but ade-quate road, left the viridian levels of the river plain, and wound its way between slopes of forest and cascades of rock rich with mountain flowers. The gradient increased steadily. The peaks had abandoned them, they were tangled in the intimacy of the foothills, and there were no longer any dis-tances before them or behind.

They emerged at last on to a broad, well-made road that crossed them at right-angles, and went snaking away left and right along the shoulder of the range.

" Which way now?"

" Whichever you like," offered Tossa with deceptive impartiality. " This must be the Freedom Road. Left is the highest end, and we're quite near it here. How about going up there to Strba Lake for lunch, and then we can drive the length of the road to Tatranská Lomnice at the other end, and see if we can go up the funicular?"

It sounded a reasonable programme, and they accepted it readily. The great road climbed still, between slopes of noble pines, until it brought them out suddenly on a broad, open terrace, and the whole panorama of the plain below expanded before them, an Olympian view of earth. They parked the van in a large ground thoughtfully provided opposite the terrace, and rushed to lean over the railing, and marvel at the pigmy world from which they had climbed.

The whole flat green valley of the Váh lay like a velvet carpet beneath them, shimmering coils of cloud drifting between. Through this wispy veil they could see clearly the white ribbon of the road, and the silver ribbon of the river, threading the emerald field, and the little towns splayed like daisies in the grass of a meadow.

"But wait till we go up to the Lomnice Peak!" Tossa promised them, and the magic of joy had penetrated even Tossa's absorption, and made her eyes shine and her voice vibrate. "This, and another leap on top of it—an enormous one, it looks in photographs. Quick, lock the van, and let's go in to the lake."

The snow-peaks, exquisitely shaped, bone-clean, polished granite and gneiss, reappeared as soon as they turned inward to the heart of the range, head beyond beautiful head materialising as they walked the curves of the road towards the blue gleam of the lake in its oval bowl. First there were white villas and large modern hotels, and then as the water opened before them broad and gracious, the older hotels, partly timbered, marking their age by their wooden towers and little lantern turrets, an element of fantasy that turned out later, surprisingly, to be traditional; for these towers for tourists were the lineal descendants of the timber churches and belfries of Slovakia, some as old as the thirteenth and fourteenth centuries.

There were hotels round almost a quarter of the lake

shore, but above and beyond rose the mountains, forested in their lower reaches, sharpened to steel above, etched with piercing patterns of ice, and snowfields radiant as flowers. Across the water, not far from the shore, towered the timber structure of a ski-jump, like an out-of-season shrub barren in summer and simulating death.

They walked the whole circuit of the lake, staring, exclaiming, photographing, as hordes of other holiday-makers, probably of a dozen nationalities at least, were also doing all round them. And Tossa took stock of every hotel they passed, and gave no sign of seeking or finding.

Not until they came to the Hotel Sokolie, built out to the very edge of the lake, with a terrace overhanging the clear, chill shallows, a sunken garden between its walls and the road, and its name on a wooden sign by the gate.

"This looks nice," said Tossa, loitering. "And not too posh, either, so it won't be frantically dear. Anybody but me hungry yet?"

She was learning how to do it. She had the tone just right, happily casual, attracted but easy, willing to go along with the general vote. She had known all along which hotel she was looking for; and that was information she could not have got from Dana.

Not one of the luxury models, just as she had said. Not even new. Half its structure was in wood, with a shingled steeple on one corner. But it had a pleasant, welcoming foyer, and a pine-panelled dining-room with a view over the terrace and the lake. And it was very easy to get the twins compliantly through the swing doors after her, and heading, on the head waiter's prompt and agile heels, towards a table near the window, where the mountains leaned to them in silver outline against a sapphire sky, and the ice-cold mountain water mirrored that blue with a deeper, gentian tone, drowning their senses, soothing them into hungry complacence.

There wasn't a hotel anywhere round the lake that couldn't have provided them with an equally wonderful prospect and a comparable menu; but only this one would

do for Tossa. For this was undoubtedly the hotel where
Herbert Terrell had stayed for his few meagre days, before
he removed to the Low Tatras, to Zbojská Dolina, and the
death that was waiting for him there.

::   ::

" I knew it!" said Toddy, groaning. " We're going to
get the English expert let loose on us wherever we go, I can
see that. And I'll swear we never actually said a word in
the head man's hearing, he just looked us over. How *do*
they know?"

" You'd be even more annoyed," said Christine with certainty, " if they took you for something else, instead. Like
all the English!"

The head waiter had led them to their table himself, but
having weighed them up in one shrewd glance he had
thereupon withdrawn, and despatched to them a short,
square, good-humoured citizen who greeted them, inevitably, in very competent English. Pretence was useless;
they were immediately recognisable, it seemed, wherever
they went.

Tossa followed the waiter's bouncing passage through the
service doors with a narrowed and speculative glance, the
gleam of purpose in her eye. She was here after information,
she had an obvious use for an English-speaking waiter. The
chief difficulty confronting her now must be how to slip her
three companions long enough and adroitly enough to be
able to talk to the man alone.

" We could have our coffee on the terrace," she suggested,
her eyes dwelling dreamily on the blue, radiant water outside.

Of course, coffee on the terrace! And then, when they
were comfortable and somnolent in the sun, half drunk with
mountain air even before they succumbed to the " Divcí
Hrozen," Tossa would begin delving into that all-purpose
bag of hers for her powder compact, and wander off
demurely into the hotel, ostensibly in search of a mirror and
privacy, but in reality in pursuit of the English-speaking
waiter.

Everything happened just as he had foreseen. At the edge of the terrace, leaning over the brilliant clarity of the water, Tossa was the first to finish her coffee, and the first to excuse herself.

"Oh, lord, what do I look like?" She peered into an inadequate mirror, and scowled horribly. "You might *tell* a girl!" She gathered up her bag in that armed, belligerent way women have, and pushed back her chair. "I'll be right back."

He gave her three minutes before he followed her in through the now almost deserted dining-room, and into the foyer. The sunken garden must, he calculated, continue past all the rooms on the landward side of the house, including lounge and bar, and not a window would be closed on a day like this. The English-speaking waiter was not in the dining-room; he might be in the bar, he might be in the kitchen, he might be almost anywhere, and out of Tossa's reach, but at least the available rooms could be covered. Dominic was launched on a course from which he could not and would not turn back. If he had to listen from hiding he would do it, yes, or at keyholes if necessary; anything to feel that he had the knowledge to help Tossa when the need arose. If it never arose, so much the better, she need never know; and nobody else ever should.

The garden was green, shrubby and wild, its lawns scythed instead of mown, as was the custom here. The thick, clovery grass swallowed his footsteps, and the level of the windows just cleared his head. He walked softly the length of the wall, listening for Tossa's voice; and suddenly there it was, clear, urgent and low, sailing out from the open window above him.

"But *why* should he leave like that? *Something* must have happened. Didn't he say anything to account for it?"

"No, madame, nothing at all." A slightly beery bass, rich and willing to please. "All was as usual with him that morning, only the rain kept him indoors. Here he sat and waited, and read the English papers. There was nothing."

" But there were other people here. Did he talk to any-one?"

"Only to me, madame. I was on duty here." The waiter's voice was patient, puzzled and reserved. Did she really think she could run round the district like this, asking fierce questions about the sudden death of a foreigner, and not call attention to herself? " We had not many callers, because of the rain. Only residents. There were a few, of course. Some herdsmen came in, local people, and drank coffee. They were playing cards, the English gentleman went over and watched them for a while. He was asking me about the pack they used, and the game they played. You have other games, this was strange to him. When the men left he picked up the paper on which they had been keeping the score, and examined it. But what is there in that?"

" But then very soon he packed and left?"

"About half an hour afterwards I saw him come down with his bag, and go to pay his account. He asked me about getting a car." The note of constraint had become a softer, more deliberate intonation of wonder and interest. He went on answering questions almost experimentally. To see what she would ask next?

"But he was interested? In these herdsmen and their game? Did you see this paper with the score on it? Was there anything special about it? But how could there be!" said Tossa hopelessly, and heaved a long, frustrated sigh.

" I did not see it, madame. He put it in his pocket and took it away with him."

The silence was abrupt and deep, like a fall down a well, but not into darkness. After a moment Tossa said, in an eased voice : " I believe his widow came and collected all his things. You don't know . . ." She drew back suddenly and warily from what she had been about to ask him, and said instead : " He asked you about the men, too? What about them?"

" Simply who they were, from what place they came. I think he was interested in the dress. The two older men wore the old, traditional dress from Zdiar."

" And which of them was the one keeping the score?"

" Oh, that was a young man I know well, but not from here, he comes from across the valley."

" Did you tell Mr. Terrell about him, too?"

" I think he asked me his name, and where he came from, yes."

In the same muted voice, but now curiously slowed, as though she had reached the end of one stage of her journey, Tossa asked : " And what *was* his name?"

" His name," said the English-speaking waiter simply, " is Ivo Martínek. His father keeps a hut, over there in the Low Tatras."

::   ::

Dominic reached the hall in a frenzied dash, just in time to saunter convincingly into Tossa's sight as she emerged from the deserted bar. He hoped she wouldn't notice his slightly quickened breathing. Looking back from the doorway as they went out to join the twins on the terrace, he caught a glimpse of the English-speaking waiter gazing after them with a wooden face and blank eyes. He was glad to let the door swing closed between them, and hustle Tossa almost crossly away from that look.

He did not, therefore, linger to take another quick glance into the hall, or he might have seen the waiter shut himself firmly into the telephone box and begin dialling a number. But even if he had been within earshot he would not have learned much, for it was not in English that the English-speaking waiter began :

" I am speaking from the Hotel Sokolie. Comrade Lieutenant, I think you should know that there is a young English lady here who is asking many questions about the dead man Terrell."

::   ::

They drove back to the Riavka at last, drugged with mountain air and bemused with splendour. Even though the highest leap of the funicular to Lomnice Peak had been out of commission—as it so often is by reason of its extreme height and free cable—they would never forget the bleached, pure, bony world of the Rocky Lake, half-way up, and the far-away, sunlit view of the valley five thousand feet below them, or the steely, shoreless waters of the lake with the clouds afloat on their surface, incredibly clear and still in a bowl of scoured rock, its couloirs and crevices outlined in permanent snow. The mirror of winter in the dazzling sunlight of summer remained with them, a picture fixed and brilliant in the mind's eye, all the way home.

Tossa had taken a great many photographs, and talked rather more than usual. The twins had hopes of her. The time would come, they felt, when they would even cease to think of her instinctively as " poor Tossa!" After all, with a mother like she had, she'd be doing extremely well if she managed to be normal at twenty. Even better, Dominic showed distinct signs of being interested, which was exactly what Christine, at least, had had in mind. And what a day! The stone-pure, sunlit, withering summits, and then this soft but lofty valley to cradle them at the sleepy end of it!

" I have to write to my mother," said Tossa resignedly, over dinner. "At least a postcard, otherwise there'll be trouble. Stick around, I won't be long."

Whatever she did now, whether she went or stayed, talked or was silent, Dominic couldn't help finding some hidden significance in it. He was uneasy in her presence, but he had no peace at all when she was absent. After a few minutes he left the others in the dining-room, and went out to the bar to buy stamps. That, at least, was his excuse; what he really wanted was to be where he could keep a silent and unobtrusive guard on Tossa.

He could not quite bring himself to follow her upstairs; things hadn't reached that pass yet. But from the bar, with the door standing wide open on the scrubbed pine hall, he would hear her if she called. Crazy, he fretted, to be thinking in such terms; and yet she was certainly meddling in something which was of grave concern to other and unknown people, and they were all these miles from home, in territory the orthodox Briton still considered to be inimical.

Dana turned from her array of bottles behind the bar,

and gave him his stamps. She looked at him in a curiously thoughtful way, as if debating what to do about him. He was turning away when she said suddenly: "Dominic!"

"Yes?" He turned back to her, shaken abruptly by the recollection that she and her family were directly involved in this mystery of Terrell's death. Her brother, that tough, stocky young forester, burned to dull gold by the yellowing mountain sun, was the man who had kept the score in the card game at the Hotel Sokolie, and left behind him, apparently quite light-heartedly, a scrap of paper which had drawn Terrell here to his death.

"I do not know," said Dana very gravely, "what it is that is troubling Miss Barber, but I think I should perhaps tell you that to-day she thought of one more question to ask me."

"Since we came home?" His choice of phrase astonished him, yet it had come quite naturally; he couldn't think of any people in Europe with whom he'd felt so quickly at home, if it hadn't been for this distorted shadow in the background.

"Yes, since then. She asked me which room Mr. Terrell occupied while he was staying here." Her eyes were searching his face closely; he felt almost transparent before that straight, wide glance.

"And which room *did* he occupy?" His throat was dry and tight with the effort to keep his voice casual.

"The one in which you and your friend are sleeping," said Dana.

He had a feeling that she knew exactly what he was going to do, and that there was no point whatever in attempting to dissemble it or postpone it. He said: "Thank you!" quite simply, not even defiantly, and walked out of the bar and straight up the stairs. The pale, scented treads creaked; she would know every step he took. Tossa, very busy upstairs, might hear the ascending footsteps, but would not recognise them; he was only too well aware that she hadn't had any attention to spare for learning things about him. None the less, he approached his own bedroom door very softly, and turned the handle with extreme care, pushing the door open before him suddenly but silently.

Tossa, on her knees at the chest of drawers, the bottom drawer open before her, brushed the lining paper flat and shoved the drawer to in one smooth movement, swinging to face him with huge eyes wary and challenging. He saw in the braced lines of her face excitement and consternation, but no fear, and that frightened him more than anything. Then she saw who it was who had walked in upon her search, and something happened to her courage. It was not, perhaps, fear that invaded her roused readiness, but a trace of shame and embarrassment, and a faint, formidable glimmer of anger.

"Oh, it's you!" she said, too brightly. "Maybe you know where Toddy's put the big map. I thought it was here somewhere. I couldn't remember how to spell some of the names." Her breathing wasn't quite in control, but the solid, sensible note was admirable, all the same.

"It's still in the van," said Dominic, in a tone to match hers.

She got up and dusted her knees, unnecessarily, for the floor was spotless and highly waxed. "Damn! It would be. Where's the road map, then, the pocket one?"

There was no way past that solid front. He found the map for her, and let her walk out with it, and with all the honours. But when she was gone he closed the door carefully, and took the room to pieces. For whatever it was she was looking for—and he was reasonably sure of the answer to that—she certainly hadn't yet had time to find it. If, of course, it was here at all. And if it was, he wasn't going to miss it.

Nothing under the linings of the drawers; she'd reached the last one, no need to look there again. Nothing under the rugs; the crevices between the pine boards were sealed closely and impermeably. No chimney, of course, except the stack of the tiled stove in the corner. He explored the accessible area inside the metal door, and found nothing. Nothing under the pelmet of the heavy curtains. Nothing in the huge, built-in wardrobe; he examined every hanger, every board of the floor. One side of it was for hanging clothes, the other had six shelves, ingeniously and improbably filled with Toddy's few belongings. Dominic stood and looked at them glumly for a moment, and then began at the top one, and tested them all to see how tightly and immovably they fitted.

The third shelf, just at shoulder-level, stirred ever so slightly in its place.

With his left hand he eased it carefully out as far as it would go, no more than a fraction of a fraction of an inch, and with the finger-tips of his right hand he felt along the rear edge of it, running his nails deep into the crevice. Two-thirds of the way along, something rustled and stirred, dislodged a centimetre from its place. A corner of something white showed beneath the shelf. He edged it gingerly lower, and drew out a long slip of paper, carefully folded to be narrower than the thickness of the shelf, and perfectly invisible when inserted behind it.

And there it was in his hand, when he had unfolded it; four columns of figures, headed by initials, broken by periodical tottings-up, the score of an unknown card game. Nothing at all odd about it that he could see, until he realised that it was scribbled on good-quality manuscript music paper, and suddenly holding it up to the light, found the upper half of an English firm's water-mark glowing at him from the close texture.

Even then it took him a full minute to think of turning it over. On the other side was noted down, in slashing strokes by a ball pen, a few bars of music, that rushed across the paper impetuously, only to be scored through impatiently a moment later, and left hanging upon an unresolved chord. Dominic hadn't worked very hard at his piano lessons when he should have done, but he could decypher enough of this to see that it was the opening of what seemed to be a rather sombre prelude for piano. Maybe a nocturne; or maybe he was merely rationalising from the few lines of verse that

were scrawled above the abortive essay, in a passionate hand
and in good English :

Come, shadow of mine end, and shape of rest,
And like to death, shine through this black-faced night.
Come thou, and charm these rebels in my breast,
Whose raving fancies do my mind affright.

Dominic stood staring at it for a moment, recognising
Dowland, and frozen to a stillness of pure wonder at finding him here in this vehement and impersonal landscape;
those poignant, piercing words of loneliness among these
aloof and unmoved mountain outlines startled like frost at
midsummer.

Then, without stopping to reason or doubt, he marched
out of the room with the wisp of paper in his hand, and
straight to the room the girls shared. Tossa was feverishly
writing her postcard there, to have something to show for
her absence. She looked up at him warily and coldly, as at
an enemy. Whoever pursued her now was her enemy, and
must simply be prepared for the hurt, and contain it, and
go on doggedly, if he wanted to help her. Dominic laid the
slip of paper on the table in front of her, and said in a flat,
detached voice :

" I think this may be what you were looking for."

Chapter 5

THE MAN ON THE SKYLINE

She gave him one flaring glance, bright and tense at the
edge of panic, and then dropped her gaze to the torn half-
sheet of paper, and sat staring at it with painful concentration for a long minute. Once she read through the few
scrawled lines of verse and scanned the twenty bars of music
without taking in a word or a note. The second time,
frowning fiercely, she grasped at least the sense of the words,
and in a moment she turned the page, and surveyed the

columns of figures. With no change in her expression she looked up at Dominic, and stared him fairly and squarely in the eye.

He expected her to say flatly: "What is this, a joke? I wasn't looking for anything, except the map. I don't know what you're talking about." For a moment, indeed, she had intended to do just that, but when he stared back at her with that intent and sombre face, waiting for her to lie to him, and disturbed and disappointed in advance, she found that she couldn't do it. What was the use, anyhow, if she couldn't be convincing? She couldn't guess what he knew, but it was enough to make him quite sure of himself. She hadn't been aware of pursuit until now, and suddenly it seemed as if she had been running to evade him ever since they left England.

"Thank you!" she said, and with a deliberation some-what spoiled by the unsteadiness of her fingers she folded the paper away into her writing-case. She waited, and there was silence, but he didn't go away and accept his dismissal; she had never thought he would. "Now I suppose you're going to ask me why I was looking for it, and what it is?"

"I know what it is," said Dominic bluntly. "It's the paper Ivo Martínek happened to have in his pocket the day your stepfather watched him and his friends playing cards in the Hotel Sokolie. He used it to keep the score on. And I know why you were looking for it. Because your stepfather picked it up afterwards in curiosity, and got so excited about it he left the lake and came over here, to find out more about it. Where it had come from, or who owned it, or who wrote those few lines of 'Come Heavy Sleep' on it, and the few bars of music. Not Ivo, that's certain, but somebody Ivo rubs shoulders with pretty casually. Or was it that he *knew* who was involved, as soon as he saw the handwriting?"

Tossa closed her writing-case with a slam. "Have you been spying on me long?" she asked in a viciously sweet tone.

It didn't hurt as much as he'd expected, because he was ready for it; he knew how she felt, and was even disposed to be on her side. He couldn't afford to stand on his dignity, since he'd kicked it from under him, perforce, the moment Tossa's safety and well-being became more important.

" Quite a time, ever since Siegburg, when you first gave yourself away. Call it spying if you want to, I don't mind. I don't care what you call it, or how badly you think of me for it, just as long as it's effective when the pinch comes. Because if you can't see that you're running head-down into trouble," he said urgently, " for God's sake wake up! Whatever you've got on your mind, quit trying to carry it alone. What do you think friends are *for*?"

" I can't tell you anything," she said defensively, shaken by the warmth of his tone.

" All right, I'm not asking you to, not yet. I'll tell you, instead. Ever since your stepfather got killed, you've been steering us steadily towards this place. First you suggested a carnet for the van, then Czech visas, then at Siegburg you started talking about coming straight into Slovakia, here, to the Tatras. That was when I began to get the idea, and after that it wasn't so hard to follow up the later developments. Suddenly you knew about a wonderful little place in Zbojská Dolina, that you'd never mentioned before. And when we were here, you took us off the path up the valley, just at the right place to locate the spot where Terrell fell and was killed. I know, I asked Dana, last night, and she told me just what she'd told you. And then you suggested a trip over into the High Tatras, and took us straight to the right resort, the one where Terrell was staying before he moved here, and even to the right hotel. And that's something you didn't get from Dana, because she said she didn't know, and I believe her. But *you* know. You had it from somebody else, before we ever came here."

" Dana must have known," Tossa said involuntarily. " It was her brother who . . ." She caught herself up too late, jerking her head aside to evade his eyes.

" Who was there playing cards in the Hotel Sokolie, and

left behind that bit of paper? Yes, evidently Terrell noticed him, all right, but that doesn't prove he ever noticed Terrell. He was with three friends, drinking coffee and playing cards, he wasn't bothered about the foreigner who came and looked on. And in any case, you didn't ask Dana about the hotel. You didn't have to, you knew it already."

"You seem," said Tossa with a tight smile, "to be pretty well-informed yourself."

"I listen at windows. Toddy ought to have warned you."

They were beginning to hate and blame each other for the stone wall between them. He was catching her tone, and that wouldn't help anyone. He dragged the dressing-table stool across the room and plumped it down close beside her chair, and leaning forward with desperate earnestness, closed his hands hard over hers. She quivered, but she didn't draw away.

"Look, Tossa, you've got to listen to me. We're not in England now. We're in Central Europe, in a Communist country. If our people think we haven't all that much reason to trust the Czechs, how much reason do you think the Czechs have to trust us? Historically, a hell of a lot less! How do you think it would look at home, if a chap with a Czech passport came poking around one of our small towns, asking a lot of nosy questions about a death that was officially accidental, cornering waiters in hotels and trying to pump them, and searching rooms for hidden bits of paper? Just give it a thought! Yes, I *was* listening under the window, I heard you talking to the waiter. That's the only time, but I don't give a damn, anyhow, you can call it what you like. What I want is for you to stay out of trouble. The way you're going on, you're going to end up in gaol. No, wait a moment!" he checked abruptly. "Let's have it quite straight. There was one other time when I spied on you. At Zilina, when we were leaving the hotel. I saw you drop your comb-case for that fellow with the MG to pick up and return. You sent him a message that way, didn't you?"

Tossa's hands lay still in his. She looked at him helplessly, and shook her head, without vehemence this time, but no less conclusively. " I'm sorry, I can't answer questions. I can't tell you anything."

" No, I beg your pardon, I said I wouldn't ask. All right, I think you did send him a message. And he sent one back to you the same way. I know you knew him before— or at least that he knew you. Maybe he's the one who started you on this hunt. The one who told you where your stepfather stayed in Strbské Pleso. The one who told you there was something wrong about the way he died. X with diplomatic plates. And then you begin drawing attention to yourself here by asking questions all over the place! Do you seriously think an English diplomat can make a move in this country without the authorities knowing all about it? It works much the same way in any country, they *have* to know where these people are and what they're doing. Don't you see, Tossa, why you frighten me to death? If you have to go on with this, why alone? If we knew what you were after we could try to help you at least, and you wouldn't have to expose yourself even further, and make yourself more conspicuous, by having to evade us, too. Wouldn't it be better?"

" I'm sorry," she said again, her voice a little unsteady. " I can't tell you anything. I haven't said yes to any of this, you're only guessing."

" All right, I'm only guessing, but they're pretty safe guesses."

" I'm sorry, I really am sorry . . . but I can't tell you. Not won't—can't." Her hands turned suddenly in his, warmly returned his grip for a moment, and then struggled free in outraged shyness. " I don't admit to anything. You'll just have to let me take my chance."

" That's something *I* can't do," said Dominic, letting her go regretfully but hastily. He caught her eye, and the gleam of a smile passed between them, and foundered in the sea of their gravity. " Not won't—can't. I'm sticking close to you, and if you ever do want me, I'll be around."

" I shan't need you. Nothing's going to happen to me.

Do the others. . . I mean, they haven't noticed anything, have they?"

" No, I'm sure they don't realise there's anything going on. And I shan't tell them. Only you can do that."

The air between them had cleared, they could look at each other again almost hopefully, and with a new curiosity. " There isn't anything going on," she said firmly, presenting the formal untruth with the assurance that it would be understood as it was offered. " Thanks, Dominic, all the same."

" Then, look, is there anything I can do to help you? Without asking any questions? You don't have to tell me why, just what I have to do."

She looked up at him intently for a moment, a deep spark kindling in her eyes. Then she ripped open the zipper of her writing-case, and drew out from the rear pocket a four-inch square of newsprint.

"Yes! If you really mean that, there is. You can help me to find this man. He's here somewhere, in this valley or near it. Take a good look at him, so you'll know if you do see him around. And if you do, tell me." She pushed the newspaper clipping across the table to him. " I stole it from the files," she said, " the day before we left England. It was the best I could find."

Dominic noted, even before he looked at the face, that the caption had been cut off. It was sharply printed for a newspaper photograph, almost certainly from a studio portrait. A man leaned forward across a desk, his jaw propped on linked hands. He might have been about thirty-five years old; a tapered face, broad across eyes and brow, lean of cheek and long of chin, with a thin, high-bridged sword of a nose, and a cool, long-lipped, sceptical mouth. The hands linked under his chin were large, broad-jointed and calm. They looked capable of anything. Light-coloured hair drew back at high temples, duplicating the arched, quizzical line of his brows. The eyes were deep-set, probing and lonely, and looked out from the page with an aloof, almost a hostile, composure.

Dominic forgot for a moment his promise to ask no questions. "Who is he?" he asked curiously, looking up across the photograph into Tossa's face.

"By all the indications," said Tossa, grimly and quietly, "he's the man who murdered my stepfather."

: :   : :

Above the chapel on its shelf of rock there were sudden moist meadows, and a wealth of brilliant green pasture. Beyond, again, lay the final great, irregular bowl, green in the base, rimmed round on all sides with paling slopes of grass and ashen slides of scree. Laborious zigzag paths climbed to two cols, where the snag-toothed rim of rocks dipped to let them through; and all the sides of the bowl were circled by contour paths, along which the hill sheep trotted confidently, and sometimes dark-red, handsome goats, chestnut-coloured like Dominic's hair.

They had probed every corner of the valley itself, and discovered every cottage. They were known, now. One of the herd-boys brought Christine edelweiss from some secret place on the summits, and a woman at the highest cottage below the huts gave them an armful of flowers from her garden. Many of the faces were becoming familiar. But they had never yet caught a glimpse of the face in Tossa's stolen photograph.

They climbed the more northerly of the two cols, and emerged among high, windy wastes of pale turf, billowing away towards more folded valleys beyond. There were no houses in sight here, only the true open, rolling, rounded crests of the Low Tatras.

They climbed the more southerly col, and beyond the crest the path traversed a broken slope of rocks, and brought them down into a high green bowl not unlike the one they had left, but smaller and more sheltered. There was a single, isolated farm here, too remote to be incorporated in any collective, and therefore still operated privately. There were smoky brown cows in the pasture, and poultry in a paddock behind the house. A handsome old woman, tall as a man, and coiffed elaborately in lace, was scything clover

in a meadow. A middle-aged man came striding through
the yard with two large milking pails; but he was short and
gnarled like a mountain tree. A plump woman shrilled at
him from a window of the house. They saw no one else
there.

Two of them, of course, were not looking for anyone in
particular. Toddy and Christine walked and scrambled and
bathed, and sunned themselves, and saw nothing constrained or secretive in their companions. Everything was
as open and candid as the day to them.

: :   : :

They were on their way back into the highest bowl of
Zbojská Dolina, lunging down the scree, when the first
heavy, solitary drops of rain fell. Ten minutes previously the
sky had been clear and blue, now a curtain of heavy purple
was being drawn slowly over the crests behind them.

" We're going to get caught," said Toddy, and paused to
look round for the quickest way to shelter. The huts lay
nearer to the path from the other col. " Let's cut a corner.
If we traverse from here to the other track we may make it
to shelter. There's a contour path, look—it cuts off a long
run in the open."

The thin grey ribbon danced its way round the side of
the bowl, threaded a few clumps of stunted bushes at the
edge of an outcrop of rock, and balanced along the rim of a
fifty-foot face of sheer, fluted cliff. At the foot of this
expanse a shelf of rock jutted out irregularly, some twelve
to fifteen feet wide, and below that the level dropped again,
though less abruptly, sliding away down open rock and
rubble and scree into the bottom of the bowl.

They saw, when they had tramped smartly along the
sheep-path in single file, and brushed through the bushes
suddenly fragrant with the first spurt of rain, that this
whole face of the bowl, the only one scoured clear of
vegetation from top to bottom, formed a slightly hollowed
channel, a groove not much more than twenty yards wide
down the side of the basin. Where they stepped out on the
rock itself, the path was solid and not even very narrow,

but polished and sloping, so that they checked and trod carefully. Looking up on their left hand towards the crests, they could see the reason. Two or three pale slides of rubble and scree, chalk-lines on the greyer rock, converged upon this ledge, and for centuries had been sending the detritus of their weathering slithering down by this route into the valley. The ledge on which the path crossed, too narrow to check the slide, had been honed into steely glossiness by its onward passage. The broader ledge below had collected the rubble as in a saucer, stacking it up neatly in a talus against the cliff.

Toddy peered respectfully over the edge. The declivity was not sheer, after all, when seen from above, nor quite without vegetation. Apart from the centre of the slide, where the polishing of friction had smoothed away all irregularities, it would not have been impossible to climb down the slope. And there below, a pie-crust of heaped boulders and stones and dust, the talus leaned innocently against the mountainside, while its accumulated overspill of years lay desultorily about the bottom of the valley, a hundred and fifty feet below.

" Look at that ! " Toddy forgot the ominous, slow slapping of the rain for a moment, and hung staring in fascination. " Wonder how long it took to build up all that lot ? "

Christine took one quick glance below, and withdrew to the inner side of the path. " Longer than it'll take to shift it, my boy, if you miss your step."

" And do you realise the process grades all that stuff down there ? Piles it up with the boulders as a base, and the finer stuff above. I read it once in some book by Norman Douglas about the Vorarlberg. And it builds up at the steepest angle maintainable. It looks as solid as a wall, and if you blew on it the whole lot would go."

" Then don't blow. Come on, the rain's coming."

In single file they paced cautiously across the level of the rock, and came thankfully out on to terraced, coarse grass and a milder slope, where they could take to their heels and go bounding towards the huts. A soft crackle of thunder and a lipping of lightning along the crests, beneath the spreading purple cloud, nipped at their heels and drove them as corgis drive cattle. The plunge of their descent carried them lower than the highest hut, and towards the cluster below. They were still a hundred yards from them when the cloud parted with a sound like the tearing of rhinoceros hide, and the rain came down in a slashing fall.

They ran like hares. The nearest door was held wide open before them, and a long brown arm hauled the girls in. In the dark, warm, steamy interior, with the fodder-loft above one end, and rough wooden benches round the walls, six of the herdsmen were gathered already, and others came running hard on their heels, scattering water from their black felt hats and frieze capes as they shed them inside the doorway.

Broadly smiling faces loomed at them through the steamy air, weather-beaten faces of large-boned young men, seamed, teak faces of hawk-nosed old men. The entire upland population of Zbojská Dolina was gathering into shelter from the first thunderstorm of August. There could not be a better place for studying them, or a better time.

They made room for the foreigners on the most comfortable bench, close to the small iron stove. An old man with thin metal chains jingling round his hat, and the traditional cream-felt trousers still worn without affectation to his daily work, embroidered thighs and all, offered them mugs of coffee, and a young fellow brought out of his leather satchel soft, light buns filled with cream cheese and poppy-seed. The air was heavy with scent of clover and damp felt and garlic breath, and it began to feel like a party. Except that at a party you do not look steadily round at every face in the company, as Tossa was doing now, memorising their lines and measuring them against a remembered face that is not present.

They had now seen, surely, every soul who habitually frequented Zbojská Dolina. But they had not seen the man Tossa was looking for.

The rain stopped as abruptly as it had started. In a

matter of seconds, before they had realised that the drum-
ming on the roof had ceased, a finger of sunlight felt its way
in at the open door, and the tatters of cloud melted magic-
ally from half the sky. They emerged into a washed and
gleaming world, withdrawing themselves almost reluctantly
from a discussion conducted in mixed German and Slovak,
with an English word thrown in here and there, notably the
now international word "folk-lore," which the herdsmen
batted about among them with a note of tolerant cynicism
in their voices. The party clamour fell behind them, with
their own thanks and farewells, and the hut emptied.

The four of them walked in silence in the wet grass, the
eastern sky pale and clear as turquoise before them, the ring
of crests picked out with piercing sunlight beneath a still
ominous darkness to westward.

"Listen!" Christine halted, head reared. "What's
that?" She looked round the slopes of the bowl, and back
towards the huts, but the sound that had caught her ear
seemed to have no source.

Then they heard it, too; a sudden rippling, vibrating
entry on a high note, that shook down a scale into a deep,
still, slow melody, breathy and hushed, like a bass flute. Soft
and intimate, and yet from no visible source, and therefore
as distant as the summits, at least, and perhaps from beyond
them. There are sounds that can whisper across ten miles
of country, especially in mountain air, where slope gives
back the echo to slope, and even a flung human voice can
span valleys as lightly as the wind. This tune—it was a full
minute before the procession of sounds became a tune to
their unaccustomed ears—was muted and wild and sad, and
the nature of the instrument, whatever it might be, seemed
to determine that it must be slow.

"Some sort of a pipe," said Dominic. "Maybe they've
got a local version of the alphorn here. That's modal, surely,
that tune?"

"Mixolydian," said Christine. "I think! I never heard
anything like it before. That entry! Listen, there he goes
again!"

Down from its first reedy, impetuous cry span the thread of sound, and settled low and softly, like a lark dropping. Full and deep the lament sang itself out, and was gone. They waited, but it did not come again.

"That's all. What a pity!"

Tossa turned back once more, before they began to descend the valley path, and halted them again with an exclamation of delight. "Look, there go the goats!"

Sleek and dark and brilliant with rain, the chestnut goats minced daintily out of the grey of rocks along the skyline, into the beam of stormy sunlight, that turned each one into a garnet on a chain for a moment, out of it again through the narrow cleft of the southerly col, and so out of sight. Gaudy as players in a spotlight, they gleamed and passed. And after them, abrupt and tall and dazzling against the dark, a man walked into their vision.

Tiny and distant as they saw him, he filled the sky for a moment. A long, rangy figure, like most of them here, in the modified local dress that made them all look like Mirek's brigand-patriot Janosík and his mountain boys. The brief glitter like a crown on his head must be the fine chains that ringed his hat, the light streaming down his body was the sheen of his rain-soaked frieze cloak. His swinging stride carried him into the gleam and out of it without pause; and they saw clearly, bright and ominous against the dark sky, the stock of the rifle projecting over his shoulder, and the inordinately long barrel swinging momentarily into sight below his hip as he turned through the col, and vanished in a swirl of his wet cloak, leaving the stage empty.

: :   : :

Below, near the Riavka hut, it had not rained at all. The meadows were dry and bright, the cloud had passed, torn its skirts on the summits, discharged its rage there, and dissolved in its own tears.

They lay in the blonde grass at the edge of the paddock, half asleep, reluctant to go indoors. And it was there that they heard the far-off pipe again. The notes came filtering into their consciousness like music heard in a dream, so distant they were, and so faint. If they had not heard them already once that day, they would probably not have been aware of them now; and even as it was, they had been listening to them inwardly for some minutes before they realised what it was that was stroking at their senses.

Dominic lay stretched out at ease, the breeze just stirring Tossa's dark hair against his shoulder, and let his mind drift with the elusive sound rather dreamed than heard. That abrupt, cascading, improvised opening, hardly loud enough to be heard at all, and yet startling, and then the full, deep, remote air. He wondered how well Christine really knew her modes? " And ever against eating cares, Lap me in soft Lydian airs." Or Mixolydian, what's the odds? To follow the tune you had to relax and let it take you along with it, for its progress was deliberate and abstracted, running line softly into line. Not until he stopped consciously listening did he catch the form of it, and fall into the loose, plaintive cadence so smoothly that the words came of themselves.

Curious how the simplest doggerel folk-songs have a way of making themselves applicable everywhere.

> *Sometimes I am uneasy*
> *And troubled in my mind....*

Like Tossa, with her tender conscience, and her sense of obligation to a man she had cordially disliked. He turned his head softly, to study through the seeding grasses her unconscious face, turned up to the slanting rays of the sun with eyes closed, half asleep, but still anxious in her half-sleep, and still vulnerable. Her eyelids, loftily arched and tenderly full, were veined as delicately as harebells, and her mouth, now that she wasn't on guard, was soft and sad and uncertain as a solitary child's.

> *Sometimes I think I'll go to my love*
> *And tell to her my mind.*

He was leaning cautiously over her on one elbow when she opened her eyes, looked up dazedly and blindingly into his face, and smiled at him without reserve or defence, out of the charmed place of her half-sleep. And suddenly, in the same instant that her open acceptance of him made his heart turn over, the true significance of his own ramblings stung his mind. He rolled over and sat bolt upright, his fingers clenched into the grass.

> Sometimes I am uneasy
> And troubled in my mind. . . .

He wasn't mistaken. That was the air he'd been hearing now for two minutes at least, and he'd known it, and never grasped what it meant, or how downright impossible it was. The pastoral mood was right, the loose form was right, and the music was certainly modal; but how could some shepherd piper here in the Low Tatras, in the heart of Central Europe, be playing an unmistakably English folk-song called " Bushes and Briars "?

Chapter 6

THE MAN IN THE CHAPEL

The astonishing thing was that no one else had noticed anything odd; they lay placidly chewing grass-stems on either side of him, and gave no sign. Nobody but himself had caught and identified the air; and in a moment more it was gone, and even the distances were silent.

He debated uneasily whether he ought to call Tossa's attention to his discovery, but the decision was taken out of his hands. He had no opportunity to speak to her alone before they were called in to their early supper; and midway through the pork and dumplings Dana appeared in the doorway to announce in a flat, noncommittal voice : " Miss Barber, someone is asking for you on the telephone."

Tossa dropped her fork with a clatter, suddenly jerked back into her private world of pitfalls and problems. Her face was tight and wild for an instant.

" *Telephone*?" said Toddy incredulously. " What, here? What secret contacts have you got in these parts, Operator

007-and-a-half?" Dominic was beginning to marvel and chafe at the insensitivity of Toddy; he'd known the girl for years, he should have felt some response to her unbearable tension.

" Don't be an ass," said Tossa with a sigh, getting to her feet with a creditable pretence of boredom and resignation. " It'll be my mother, of course."

No one, fortunately, thought fast enough to observe that they had come to Zbojská Dolina only on the spur of the moment, and their address certainly could not be known to anyone in England, since Tossa's card home had been posted only yesterday.

" I never thought your fond mama was fond enough to spend a guinea a minute, or whatever it is, talking across Europe to her darling daughter," said Christine cynically.

" Don't be silly, Paul will be paying the bill, of course."

Dana, hovering in the doorway, said clearly and deliberately : " It is a man calling." She cast one brief glance at Dominic, and hoisted her shoulder in a slight but significant shrug. She was a little tired of secrecy, and not altogether disposed to go on being discreet. Dana was taking no more responsibility for anything or anyone. It was up to him now.

" What did I tell you? Paul getting paternal!" Tossa walked away to take her call, the back view almost convincing, resigned and good-humoured, ready to report faithfully to her demanding family, and extricate herself from any further enquiries. Though of course, she knew, none better, that it was not Chloe Terrell on the line, or Paul Newcombe, either, or anyone else in far-off England, but somebody here in Slovakia, somebody from whom she had been half expecting a message all this time.

She came back a few minutes later, still admirably composed, if a little tense. She sat down with a sigh, and resumed operations hungrily on her pork and dumplings.

" Everything all right?" asked Christine cheerfully.

" Oh, sure, everything's all right. They're home, and no troubles. Just felt they ought to check up on the stray lamb." She wasn't too loquacious, because she never talked much about her relationship with her mother, and it wouldn't ring true now. "Paul mostly, of course, they're always like that. He means well."

When she was lying with every word and every motion of her body she could still, it seemed, keep the secret from the Mather twins, but she couldn't keep it from Dominic. A private geiger-counter built into his deepest being started a pulsating pain in response to the rising of the hackles of her conscience, and halved her pain. And she was aware of it, for she flashed one appraising look at him, and then resolutely evaded his eyes.

But repeatedly, he noticed, his senses perhaps sharpened by the pain, she was glancing now at her watch. She had an appointment to keep? Or she was counting the minutes until she could be alone and stop lying? It wasn't her natural condition, it hurt her badly, she might well look forward to a respite from it.

But no, she had an appointment! She drank her coffee quickly, though it was scalding hot. She had one eye constantly on the time, and was calculating something in her mind, and frowning over it.

"You won't mind if I run off and write a proper letter home?" she said deprecatingly, pushing her chair back. "It's the one sure way to keep 'em quiet for the rest of the trip."

"You could do it down here," suggested Toddy obtusely, "and nod our way occasionally."

"What, with television around? You don't know how much concentration it takes. I'll be down in an hour or so."

She made her escape in good order; only the back view, as she left the room, somehow conveyed a sense of brittleness, excitement and tension. But she was right, they had television to divert their minds, compulsive here even before the sun was down, because they were on holiday from all cerebral engagements, because they had been out in the fresh air all day, and because, when it came to the point, the programmes were rather better than at home, and the picture very much better. They wouldn't begin to miss Tossa for an hour or so, and they wouldn't miss him, either.

He gave her two minutes start; he was afraid to make it longer. Then he made an easy excuse about bringing down the maps and surveying the route into Levoca, where there was a notable church and some splendid carving by Master Paul. They agreed cheerfully; they would have agreed to anything, provided it made no claim on them to-night.

He walked straight through the bar, across the terrace, and out to the edge of the trees. There he waited, because the light was still on in the girls' room. If she didn't come in a few more minutes, he would assume he could relax, and think about fetching the maps. And he would feel crazily happy to be owing her an apology; as though she wronged him by going her own way, and he injured her by feeling injured. The relationship between them was growing more and more complex and painful.

The light in the girls' room went out.

He counted the seconds, hoping she wouldn't come, ready to blame himself for all sorts of suspicions to which he had no right. Then he saw Tossa's slight, unmistakable shape in the doorway, saw her close the door behind her and slip away from the house, heading towards the climbing path.

He stood motionless among the trees, and let her pass. It was still daylight, though the direct rays of the sun had forsaken the valleys, and were fingering hesitantly at the heights. In the bowl among the summits, where the chestnut goats habited with their elusive bandit-herdsman, it would still be broad day; here among the trees it was almost dusk already. She had the evening world to herself; she moved through it like a wraith.

Dominic stole out of his hiding-place and silently followed her.

: :   : :

Among the trees it was easy to keep relatively close to her, and still escape notice; but afterwards, when they came to the heath land and the scattered rocks, through which the track threaded bewilderingly, he had to hang back a little and slip from cover to cover with care. If she looked back at a turn of the path she might easily glimpse him, and he was reluctant to be caught shadowing her, however illogical that might seem. She hadn't made any concessions, hadn't invited him into this secret affair of hers, hadn't asked him for anything. She had given him her commission without her confidence, and only when he asked for it; and his acceptance of it had given him no rights whatsoever, because he had bargained for none. But neither had he made any promises to withdraw, or cede any of his rights to act on his own. Principal and shadow, they maintained each his station. But he felt that there was, in a way, an obligation on him not to obtrude.

The bruised grasses underfoot, rich with dwarf heaths and wild thyme, sent up a heady sweetness in the cooling evening, and the small breeze that came with the change brought back to him the occasional light rustle of Tossa's shoes on the loose stones. The most difficult bit was going to be the belt of open meadows, before the valley closed in on both sides in broken rock faces and drifts of rubble and scree, mingled with scattered copses and thickets of bushes. How far could she be going? Not up to the highest bowl, surely, where the huts were? At this hour, and without a coat?

She was out of the rock belt now, she set off boldly across the meadows, and he hung back in cover, and let her go. Once she looked round, and stood for a moment with head reared, watching and listening to make sure she was alone. Then, satisfied, she turned and hurried on, breaking into a run.

He dared not step into the open after her until she had vanished at the first turn of the path, where the outcrop rocks closed in upon it and twisted it, like fingers snapping off a thread. But then he set off across the thick, silent turf at a fast run, to make good the distance he had lost. Even if she looked back, now, she could not see him, and with this springy carpet under his feet she would not hear him. He reached the rocks, and began darting after her from bend to bend of the cramped path, until he heard a stone roll away from under her foot, somewhere ahead of him and not far away.

She had left the path; though narrow and winding here, it was almost level and partly grassed, a stone would not roll like that unless she had begun to climb again. By the sound, she had turned to the right from the track. That way there was at least one possible goal; he could see the roof of the little refuge, rose-coloured tiles against the backdrop of ashen scree. It was still in sunlight, a long ray pierced the open lantern tower like a golden lance. They had climbed a considerable distance already, and for a little while, at least, had outdistanced the twilight.

Yes, she was heading for the chapel. Quiet as she was, the small sounds she did make came down to him clearly, and he could trace her progress by them. The pathway up to the shelf had been laid, at one time, with flat stones, but many of them were unsteady now. And here there were thick bushes and even trees, encouraged by the shelter of the little promontory. Stones from the encroaching scree-slope behind had rolled right down among the bushes, and lay raw and pale in the grass. Then, as the track reached the edge of the level shelf, the trees fell back, and Tossa stepped out on to the plane of rock before the chapel door. Rubbish of scree had reached the wall on the inner side, and begun to pile up against the footings.

Tossa never hesitated. She walked quickly across the few yards of open space, towards the door that sagged sideways on its broken hinge. Dominic wormed his way to the edge of the trees, and watched her go. The place seemed private, silent and abandoned, surely safe enough. He found himself a secure spot in cover, and settled down to wait until she should reappear.

Tossa reached the door, laid her hand on the leaning timbers, and slid round them into the chapel. It seemed she might be a few minutes late for her appointment; at any rate, it was three minutes past eight by Dominic's watch. She vanished. He began, almost unconsciously, to count seconds.

Four seconds, to be exact. Four seconds of silence from the instant when she disappeared round the sagging door into the dark interior. Then the sharp, small crack, that he took first for a dry twig snapping under a foot, and knew next moment for a gun-shot.

He discovered that he knew it when he found himself flat on his face, writhing like an eel out of the bushes and on to the grey, striated face of rock, wriggling frantically towards the door of the chapel. And it seemed that his senses were capable of splitting themselves into action squads, where the need was sharp enough, for he was simultaneously aware of recording the dull sound of a fall, and the faintest of muted cries, while his conscious hearing was busy with the sound of the shot, struggling to sort out its direction, and baffled by a multiplicity of echoes. Here in this confined and complex valley every explosion of sound ricocheted from plane to plane, repeated endlessly along the gorge, out to the open bowl to westward, and the lowland spaces to eastward.

Tossa had walked into the chapel erect and innocent. Dominic crawled, drawing up his feet behind him into the grateful shade of the doorway, and dragging himself up by the great iron latch. He scrambled round the obstruction, and the first thing that hit him was the slanting shaft of sunlight through the empty window-frame on his left hand. It blinded him for a moment, and then, before he regained his sight or took his sheltering arm down from his eyes, he grasped the significance of this late radiance, and dropped to the floor again in a hurry. His outstretched right hand lit upon something warm and rough-textured, a tweed sleeve, the roundness of an arm limp and still within it.

A yard before his face, and on the same level, Tossa's face hung frozen and blank with shock, lips parted, great eyes stunned into dullness. That was the first thing he saw as his vision cleared again. The second was the young man who lay sprawled between them half on his face, one arm doubled under him, one flung out towards the doorway, with a blue-black hole oozing a sluggish glue of blood just to the right of the base of his skull, in the neatly cropped fair hair, and a small pool gathering underneath his throat, in the dust of the paved floor. A well-dressed young man, in good grey slacks and sportscoat, as English as brown ale. It was hardly necessary to stoop and examine the motionless, astonished face pressed against the dirty flagstones, but Dominic did it, all the same.

The man who ran the MG, the man who had drunk coffee in a corner of the kavárna at Zilina, and exchanged messages with Tossa by means of her comb-case, was never going to report on his mission, whatever it might be. There was no pulse detectable in the wrist on which Dominic pressed his fingers; there was not the faintest misting discernible on the watch-glass he held to the slack lips for want of a mirror.

X with diplomatic plates was unmistakably and irrevocably dead.

: :   : :

Tossa came out of her daze with a violence that almost shattered them both, broke into rending, tearless sobs, and tried to get to her feet, in a horrified recoil from the poor creature on the floor. Dominic dropped the heavy hand he had been holding, and caught her by the shoulders roughly, pulling her down again.

"Don't get up! Don't you understand? The window! The light!" He reached across the dead man, and drew her close to him, kneeling upright and holding her tightly in his arms. His back ached with her weight and his own, but that didn't matter. Neither, for the moment, did the dead man over whom they leaned to each other thankfully and fearfully. "I'm here, I'm with you, I won't leave you. Keep down, and keep hold of me. You'll be all right. Tossa, you know me—Dominic. Now, take it easily, and we'll pull out all right. I came to look after you. I said I'd be around."

"He's dead!" whispered Tossa, shivering with shock.

" He *is* dead, isn't he? There's nothing we can do for him?"

" No, there's nothing we can do. He's dead." It disposed, he saw, of the first urgency. He felt her relax in his arms. Now they were two, burdened with the responsibility only for themselves. It was no comfort at all, but it simplified things. It even accelerated understanding.

" I came here to meet him," she said numbly. " He telephoned me. It wasn't my mother."

" I know. Never mind that now. What happened? When you came in here? Tell me what you can."

" He was standing over there," she said in a dulled but obedient whisper, " beyond the window, where it's dark. When I came in, he started across to meet me. He stepped right into the sunlight, and then he suddenly lurched forward, and fell past me. I couldn't understand what had happened to him, all at once like that."

" Somebody shot him," said Dominic. " Somebody's outside with a rifle. I heard the shot. He was covering that window, waiting for his chance, and he got it when this chap stepped into the light. So keep down here in the shadow, whatever you do."

" He may have seen us come," she said, shuddering in his arms, " you or me or both. Especially me—I didn't hide. Suppose he thinks Mr. Welland may have told me something before he was killed? He *came* to tell me something!"

" Somebody out there was damned determined he shouldn't get the chance. *Did* he manage to say anything to you? Anything at all?"

" When I came in he started to say : ' Miss Barber, there you are.' Something like that. And then he pitched forward and fell down."

" And afterwards? When you were kneeling by him?"

" He did try to say something. It sounded like : ' But he couldn't have known—nobody else knew!' And then he said : ' Impossible!' quite clearly, sort of angrily. Just : ' Impossible!' And then there wasn't anything else. And now he's dead!"

"And on the telephone? He didn't tell you anything then?"

"He only said he must see me, and would I meet him here. It's my fault. If it hadn't been for me, if I hadn't interfered, he'd still have been alive. I never wanted to break things, but I do. I break everything!"

She was shaken by a momentary gust of weeping, but she pushed the weakness away from her indignantly, and clung to Dominic's sweater with convulsive fingers, as to the anchor of her sanity.

"If the man outside—the man with the rifle—if he knows we're in here, if he knows we're defenceless, we're as good as dead, too, aren't we? Because he can't afford any witnesses."

"He may not know. And even if he does, he can't be all sides of us at once. Listen, Tossa! You stay here, and stay down. You understand? I want to take a look out of the window."

"You can't! He's that side, he must be. He'll fire again." She kept her hold of him fiercely, and it was not a hysterical grip, but a very practical and determined one, meant to secure what she valued.

"Don't worry, I'm not going to show myself, I'm not such a fool. I've got to see where he could be, and how much ground he can cover." He detached her hands from his person firmly, and slid away from her along the dusty floor, to draw himself up cautiously on the dark western side of the window.

With his cheek flattened against the wall, he could peer out with one eye over the range of country which must contain, somewhere, the man with the rifle trained on this spot. He found himself looking out, as he might have realised before if his mind had been working normally, over the full width of the valley, for below him the ground fell away to the path and the brook. Only a long segment of the opposite wall of the valley was presented to view. That was comforting, for it meant the marksman must be some considerable distance away, too far to change his ground quickly.

His field of fire was more or less determined. Dominic recollected the way the bullet had entered, slightly to right of centre near the base of the skull. That seemed to indicate that the rifleman was somewhat up-valley from their position, undoubtedly somewhere in cover on the far side, and approximately on a level with the chapel.

Right opposite the window where he stood, and on a level perhaps a few yards higher, was the scarred face of rock where Herbert Terrell had fallen to his death. There were plenty of bushes at the up-valley side of that cliff-face. The position was approximately right. Murder, it seemed, clung very close to this spot.

What could the distance be? Nearly half a mile, surely. Did that mean telescopic sights? If he couldn't sight them from where he was, he certainly couldn't change his position and shorten the range very quickly. And if he was covering this window from over there, he couldn't even see the doorway, it was round a good, solid corner of masonry. So with a lot of luck he might not have seen them at all. In that case he could only feel uneasily certain that the young man who knew too much must have come here to meet someone, and he might, just might, know enough to feel sure who that someone was likely to be. But he couldn't *know*, at this moment, and he couldn't break cover and show himself, *in case* someone escaped to tell the tale. Secrecy was of the essence. When he killed it had to be anonymously, unless he could be absolutely sure of killing *everyone* who might be able to connect him with the affair.

There was cover for most of the way back to the Riavka hut; only the thirty yards of open rock here outside the door, and the expanse of meadows well below, presented real hazards. And the first was surely the worst, just the getting out of this stone box, and into the bushes. It was all very well calculating hopefully that the enemy must be in a position from which he ought not to be able to see the doorway, but even so he might be able to see the last few yards of that rock shelf before the path dropped from it into the trees. And it appeared that he was an excellent shot, too

good by half. Could he command a view of the lower
meadows from his perch? And would a target crossing
them be still within his range?

If they waited a little while the abrupt dusk would fall,
and make it easier to move unseen; but easier for their
enemy as well as for them. And in that same little while he
could be down in the valley, if he knew enough to be sure
who they were and where they must make for, and slicing
diagonally across rough ground to get to the meadows before them and cut them off there.

Dominic licked sweat from his lip, and hung irresolute for
a moment. The slanting shaft of sunlight, narrower and
narrower every moment, had begun to tilt steadily now.
The globule of brightness where it struck the far side of the
window-frame was climbing upwards, accelerating all the
time. He understood; the sun had reached the point of
dropping behind the crests, and when the last sliver of
orange-red vanished it would suddenly be half-dark. If
there was going to be one moment when it would be safe
to run across the shelf of rock and into the trees, that would
be the moment. The valley dusk fell like a stone; even
eyes braced and trained to watch steadily must be blind for
a second or two.

He looked down at Tossa, coiled in the dust of the floor
and watching him unwaveringly. She had on a heather
tweed skirt that could vanish against almost any indeter-
minate background, but her sweater was cream-coloured.
Dominic peeled off his dark-red pullover, and tossed it
across to her.

" Put this on. And for God's sake do just what I tell you,
and don't give me an argument. We've got to get out of
here intact, that's all that matters."

She looked at the dead man, and said faintly: " We
can't leave him here like this."

" Don't be an idiot! We can't take him with us, and if
we get knocked off ourselves we can't even report his death.
Do as I tell you. Put that pullover on, and get over to the
door. Stay inside until I give you the word, and then run

for the trees. And I mean *run*! And keep running. Stay in cover. When you come to the open bit, I hope it'll be dark enough to cover you, but run like a hare, anyway. Don't stop till you get home. I'll be following you."

The globule of gold, redder and angrier now, was half-way up the window-frame, and gliding upwards always a shade more rapidly. Tossa scrambled into the dark pull-over, and slid like a cat along the flagstones, but towards him, not away from him. Before he knew what she was about she was on her feet close to him, trembling against his shoulder.

He turned on her furiously. "Get the hell over to the door, I told you! . . ."

He broke off there, confounded. In the half-darkness her soiled, strained face was only inches from his own, and not fixed in ill-judged obstinacy, as he had expected, but utterly grave and calm. It was as if he had never seen her eyes fully alive and conscious before, because what she was looking at now was the intimate prospect of death.

"Yes, I'm going," she said placatingly, and leaned for-ward suddenly the last few inches, stretching on tip-toe. Her mouth touched his hesitantly, fixed and clung for a staggering instant. "Just in case!" she said in a rushing whisper, and she was gone, stooping and darting under the wasting finger of light, and crouching alert and still just within the doorway.

The circle of gold reached the top of the window-frame, and collapsing together like a punctured balloon, vanished. The glow went out, the dusk came down like a lid.

"Now!" urged Dominic hoarsely. "*Run*!"

She was off like a launched arrow. He heard the light, rapid flurry of her footsteps racing across the smooth rock, heard them recede, vibrating away into silence. He held his breath until the blood thundered in his ears, waiting for the shot, but it didn't come. She was away safely, she hadn't been seen.

His knees shook under him with relief and reaction. He clung to the edge of the window and leaned his forehead against the chilly, flaking whitewash of the wall for a moment. Now give her time, don't follow her too soon, in case *he* makes some move to case the chapel more closely. Because he must be wondering desperately how successful he's been, whether this poor devil's mouth is securely closed, and whether it was closed in time. There must be no more disturbances, here round the chapel, until Tossa's clear away and safely out of it.

He laid the back of his hand against his lips, carefully and wonderingly, pressing the lingering warmth and stupefaction of her kiss more intimately into his flesh. It would be a mean thing, as well as a stupid one, to attach too much significance to it. She'd kissed Mirek when he left them. Dominic was beginning to understand that action of hers very well now; it was an act of atonement for the distrust she had felt of Mirek's disinterested kindness. And she'd kissed him now out of gratitude just for his being there, and as a symbol of human solidarity, in the face of the threat to their lives. And that was all. An impulse, like the other one, because she was not very articulate, even if there'd been time for words.

Five minutes, at least, before he ought to move to follow her, and nothing now he could do, except watch that darkening expanse of mountain-side across the valley, and listen with strained ears for any sound. She would be among the rocks now, near the edge of the meadows. Thank God she could run like a deer. And the man with the gun was half a mile away, even as the crow flies, and nearer a mile on the ground. Out of his sight was out of his reach.

But what had she meant by: " Just in case!"? The words penetrated to his brain only now, and shook him with a new astonishment, and a new and illuminating recollection of her face, half out of focus because of its nearness, reaching up to his. He had never seen her utterly relaxed and at rest until that moment; as though she had only just seen clearly what it was all about, and what was of value in it, and what of no value, and dropped all the non-essentials, like worrying about her own conscience, to concentrate on what really mattered. And kissed you, he said to himself sardonically. My boy, you fancy yourself!

Detail was lost now in a dimness which was not yet dark —the afterglow was something for which he hadn't, in fact, made sufficient allowance—but which did confuse vision over any distance. The five minutes were up, surely he could risk leaving now. If he attracted notice, at least she was clear of it, there was one safely away to raise the alarm. And since Tossa had crossed the open space without producing any reaction, the odds were that his original calculations had been accurate, and that whole shelf of rock before the doorway was out of the murderer's range. No harm, though, in making a run for it.

He stepped wincingly round the body stretched on the dusty floor, and for a moment the thought of leaving him here alone was almost unbearable. Death is lonely enough in any case. He had never seen it quite so close before, and never so crudely, only in its tamed and mitigated state, ringed with rites and sympathisers. Dominic stood shivering for a moment in his thin sweater-shirt, irresolute over the dead man, and then turned his head aside with determination, and made for the door. The only thing he could do for this poor wretch was not to be done here. He slid round the leaning door, stepped out gingerly on to the rock, and ran.

Half-way across the open space a stone rolled under his foot, and brought him down in a heavy fall, knocking the breath out of him. The noise seemed enormous, and set echoes rolling from side to side of the valley. He lay half-dazed, but already groping forward with his hands to thrust himself to his feet again; and suddenly a second sharp, dry crack sent sharper echoes hiccuping down the rocks, and something hit the ground close beside his right ear with a horrid leaden plunk and a sharp, protesting whine.

Every nerve in him curled wiltingly in upon itself, struggling to make him smaller and less vulnerable. Every particle of energy he had left in him gathered him to his

feet in a wild leap, and hurled him forward towards the
shelter of the trees. He knew very little about guns, but he
knew the whimper of a bullet ricocheting. Not an inch of
this shelf was out of the marksman's range now, and a
racket like that fall, to a true ear, made almost as fair a
target as a proper sighting. He *had* changed his position,
but he was still up there on the hillside, he'd merely worked
his way down-valley on the same level, to cover the doorway. By the only route, then—by the traverse path across
the cliff, from which Terrell had fallen to his death.

Dominic reached the edge of the trees and half-fell into
their shelter; and something flew out of the green shade to
meet him, and folded thin, straining arms about him with
a sob of thankfulness and desperation. The shock fetched a
gasp out of him. He clasped the embracing fury tightly,
and hissed at her in confused rage:

"What the hell are you doing here? I told you to keep
going!"

"Without you?" Tossa spat back at him indignantly.
"What do you take me for?"

"Well, come on now, damn you! Get out of here,
quick!"

"My God, I like that! I've only been waiting for
you!"

"Shut up, just *run*!"

He caught her by the wrist, and dragged her at a frenzied, slithering run down the steep path. Speed was better
than silence, now that they were in cover. Whatever noise
they made they could out-distance, and the man with the
gun, whatever his powers as a shot, had just demonstrated
that he was still up there on the opposite mountainside, and
could not possibly out-run them on their way down to the
hut. Behind them they heard the sound of stones rolling,
the faint slither of scree. Perhaps the spent bullet had
started a minor slide. They didn't stop to investigate. Hand
in hand they ran, untidily, blindly, bruising themselves
against rocks, slipping on the glossy grass, until they reached
the main path, and settled down to a steady, careful run.

Across the meadows they could race silently, the thick turf swallowing their footsteps; and beyond, through the broken heathland, they relaxed their speed a little, feeling themselves almost safe, almost home.

"Dominic—he didn't hit you? You're sure?"

"No, I'm all right, he didn't hit me. But, Tossa . . ."

"Yes?"

"We can't keep quiet now. This is murder. You'll have to tell everything you know."

"I can't! You don't understand."

"You'll *have* to tell how this happened. If you don't I shall. And it was to him you promised not to tell anything —wasn't it?"

"Yes," she said faintly. They were in the darkness of the forest now, above the brook, and they had to go gently, partly because they found themselves suddenly very tired and unsteady, partly because the path was narrow and the night deeper here. He folded his arm about her, and they moved together, warmly supporting each other.

"He's dead, Tossa. It's for him you have to tell the truth, now. That releases you."

"No," she said, shivering. "You don't understand. I'll tell *you*, but I can't tell people here. I can't! You'll see that I can't."

"Never mind, don't worry now. Let's get home and find the twins. We'll talk it over, we'll see how best to handle it."

Touching each other in the darkness, holding fast to each other where the path was tricky, confounded them almost more than their momentary head-on encounter with death. They were close to the deep green basin where the hut lay; the lighted windows shone upon them through the trees. Hand in hand they stumbled across the open grass towards the door of the bar.

Chapter 7

THE MAN WHO WASN'T IN CHARGE

The first look at their soiled and shaken faces effectively cut off all questions and exclamations, shocking the twins into silence. The significant jerk of Dominic's head drew them after him up the stairs, unresisting, to an urgent council of war.

In the girls' bedroom, secure from surprise at the far end of a creaky wooden corridor, Tossa sat down on her bed and unburdened herself of the whole story at last : how she had blundered into the affair by accident, through reading Robert Welland's note left for her mother, how he had come back to reclaim it, too late, and made the best of it by telling her everything, and so putting her under the sacred obligation to keep it secret. She told them everything she had learned about Karol Alda, why he must be somewhere here, close at hand, and why it was almost certain that he was a double murderer. The newspaper photograph, the half-sheet of music paper, passed from hand to hand in a stunned silence.

" I believe my stepfather recognised this handwriting as soon as he saw it in the Hotel Sokolie. He must have seen it regularly when they were both at the Marrion Institute, and it was his job not to forget things like that. I think he followed Ivo Martínek over here to look for Alda. I don't suggest the Martíneks know anything much, or even that they're particularly close to Alda. This place is an inn, the local people do use it, and that piece of paper could easily have been left here some time when Alda was here, maybe sitting over a beer, playing with an idea he had in his mind. He's a musician, too, it seems he was a very good one. He didn't get this right. He tore off the false start and left it on the table. Maybe Ivo just picked it up out of curiosity, and felt interested enough to pocket it. Something like that, something quite casual and harmless, because he didn't think twice about making use of it when he wanted a paper to score their card game, and he didn't bother to take it away with him afterwards. But it did prove Alda was somewhere in the vicinity of the Martíneks, known and accepted there. So my stepfather came to look for him here. And he was killed here, up the valley where we went the first day. Opposite the place where Mr. Welland was killed to-night."

"And for the same reason," said Toddy positively, his face sharp with excitement. "Because they both located him! Isn't it plain? This chap Welland was to try to trace him, and report back to the Institute through the embassy in Prague. And he'd done it! He was in Zilina when we came through, and saw you there, and you tipped him off where he could find you. And three days later he turns up on the telephone, asking you to meet him. He'd found him! He'd been to Prague to send the notification they'd agreed on, and he came back here to keep an eye on events in the meantime. *You* were a complication."

"My guess is," said Christine, gnawing her knuckles furiously, "he was worried about you turning up on the scene. He'd been thinking it over, and he wanted to have a word with you to-night to get you to lay off. Maybe to tell you whatever he knew, as the best way of satisfying you. But certainly to warn you not to start anything."

"Whatever he had to say to me," said Tossa, "couldn't be said over the telephone. Maybe he was going to tell me where Alda was, maybe he wasn't. What difference does it make now? Whoever killed him was taking no chances. And now what do we do?"

"We report the death," said Dominic forcibly, "and co-operate with the police."

Toddy gaped between the fists that clutched his disordered hair. "Are you crazy? Can't you see this is a hand we've got to play *against* the police? Against the Czech authorities, against every soul round us? Can't you see there's a little matter of national security involved? Tossa's told you, the affair's top secret, and big enough to kill for. She's pledged to keep everything to do with the Marrion Institute secret, and that goes for us, too."

"You're seeing this as a real-life spy thriller," said Dominic without heat. "I'm seeing it as a murder. Murder is something I don't play spy games with. Odd as it may seem to you, I believe that the professional police everywhere are dead against murder, and when they run up against it their instinct is quite simply to try to find out who did it, and get him. If you ask me, do I think that goes in a Communist country, yes, I think it goes in every country, and always will, as long as people are people and professionals are professionals. It's a queer thing about police— by and large, in spite of a few slip-ups, *they don't like crime.* And I come from a police family, and I don't like it, either. So either *we* go to the police or *I* go to the police. Whichever way you like."

"*We* go," said Tossa, faintly but finally. "We have to, I do see that. We owe it to him *and* to them. Only I can't tell everything. I can't tell about the Institute, or anything that's mixed up with security. You may be right about the police, Dom, they may be absolutely on the level. Only I'm bound, don't you see that? I'm not entitled to take any risks, it isn't for me to judge."

"You can tell them about the shooting," urged Christine, "without mentioning the background. You could say you went up the valley for a walk after dinner, and heard the shot, and found him in there. There's no need to say you went there to meet him."

"That's it! You'd be giving them everything that could possibly help them over Welland's murder. *If* they're genuinely interested in solving it," said Toddy sceptically, "though that's a laugh, if ever I heard one. You were out together, you two, you blundered into it without meaning to. That's all you need say."

"Even just to cover ourselves," admitted Christine,

frowning over the perilous tangle that confronted them, " we'd have to go that far. But there's no need to go any further. What are we supposed to do, go there and say: ' Please, some of your confidential agents have wiped out two of ours because they got too near to something hot. Do something about it!'? I like to think I'm honest, but my God, I don't take it to those lengths!"

"And supposing there's nothing whatever official or approved about this murder?" demanded Dominic. " Supposing it's a completely private act, and the police are just as interested in catching the criminal as you are. You think it'll make no difference to their chances, our keeping back nine-tenths of the facts?"

" You can't," protested Toddy savagely, " be as simple as you're acting!"

" Wish I could say the same for you, but apparently you can. All right, we can't drag the Institute into it, but we could still tell the truth about to-night, we could still say he telephoned Tossa and asked her to meet him, we could even say why—that she didn't feel satisfied about her stepfather's death, and came here to see for herself, and Mr. Welland was in her confidence and wanted to help her. Half of which," said Dominic, scrubbing at his tired forehead, still pallid with dust from the white-washed wall of the chapel, " they'll know already, and if you doubt that you're even simpler than I thought. But make up your minds, and let's get going. I'm for telling as much of the truth as we can."

"And I'm for using our gumption and telling as little as possible." Toddy set his jaw obstinately. " Didn't you hear, there are plans of secret work involved, valuable stuff, dangerous stuff. Of course it's no private murder. You just heard the shot, and went in and found him. For God's sake, whose side are you on?"

" Christine?" appealed Dominic, ignoring that.

"I'm with Toddy," said Christine, roused and belligerent. " Let's face it, we're in enemy territory over this, we *can't* co-operate."

Dominic looked down at Tossa's tormented face, and

gently touched her hand. " It's up to you, Tossa. Whatever
you say, I'll go along with."

She shook her head helplessly, and didn't look up; after a
moment she said huskily : " I can't! I'd like to. I'd much
rather, but I can't. I'm with them, Dominic."

" All right, we'll do it that way." He looked at Toddy,
who alone had enough German to be sure of communi-
cating, where none of them had Slovak, and English was
somewhat less common an accomplishment than in Prague.
" Will you telephone, please, Tod? You'll have to ask Dana
which is the right place to call, but all you have to get over
is that we're reporting a death, and where they'll find him,
and that we're coming in with our statements. We shall
have to, so why not now? Find out where we should check
in, and I'll be getting the van out."

: :   : :

Liptovsky Pavol, St.-Paul-in-Liptov, turned out to be a
small town of perhaps five short streets, all of them con-
verging on the vast cobbled square in front of the church.
Two of the streets, which were a yard or so wider than the
others, conducted the main road in and out of this imposing
open space, which in fact was not a square at all, but a long
wedge-shape, inadequately lit, completely deserted except
for two or three parked Skodas and an ingenious home-
made body on a wartime Volkswagen chassis, and scalloped
on both long sides with deep arcades, beneath which the
van's lights fingered out the glass of shop windows. The
short side of the wedge was the municipal buildings, the only
twentieth-century block in sight; and in the rear quarters
of this town hall there were two rooms which did duty as
the police office for the sub-district.

It was past ten o'clock by the time they found it, and
locked the van on the cobbles outside; but they were not
surprised to see the door open and the lights on inside the
dingy passage-way, since their telephone call would
obviously have alerted the local force, and presumably sent
someone clambering and cursing out to the chapel in
Zbojská Dolina long before this. In such a quiet little place

the police office would surely be closed and abandoned around five o'clock, at normal times.

They had agreed on the way that Dominic was to do the talking. Of the two who had been on the scene, presumably the Slovaks would expect the man to act as spokesman, the girl to confirm what he said. Even such small points affect one's chance of being believed without question.

The passage was vaulted, with peeling plaster, and belonged to some older building, now largely replaced. There was an open door at one side of it, and a steep wooden staircase within. Dominic climbed it slowly, his throat dry and constricted, every step carrying him deeper into a strange land. What if Toddy was right? What if the damned cold war was still almost at freezing point, and he was in enemy territory? He had felt nothing but friends round him here, but suddenly he was a little afraid. "He speaks English," Toddy had reported, coming back confounded from his telephone call. " *Good* English!" It had frightened Toddy more than anything else, when it ought to have reassured him and made things easier; and it was frightening Dominic now. With an interpreter you have also a protective barrier, you can plead misunderstanding, you can be inarticulate and still credible. With this man he was deprived of any insulation. But at least he was warned.

" *Pod'te d'alej*!" said a leisurely, rumbling bass voice, in reply to his tentative knock on the door at the top of the stairs. And next, in the same easy tone: "Come in, please!"

He spoke excellent English, almost unaccented. Learned from records? Certainly not only from the book.

Dominic opened the door and went in, the other three filing closely behind him. Toddy closed the door after them. The room was small, twelve by twelve at most, and bare, furnished with a couple of chairs in front of the desk, and two more behind, a battered typewriter, two tall, narrow filing cabinets, and a small, iron stove. The walls were painted a dull cream, and scaling here and there. Behind the desk somebody had used the wall as a convenient tablet for notes, calculations, and pencilled doodlings, perhaps while hanging on the telephone, or filling in very dull duty hours with nothing to do. It would be very surprising indeed if there was much crime in Liptovsky Pavol.

"*Nadporucik* Ondrejov?" asked Dominic with aching care. To the best of his knowledge the correct translation of the rank was "lieutenant," like an army rank, but he didn't feel certain enough of his facts to use it. He preferred at least to pay his host the compliment of attempting to pronounce his Czechoslovak title.

The elderly countryman behind the desk took his broad behind off the office chair, and rose to straddle the floor like a farmer his lands.

"Come in, come in! Yes, I'm Ondrejov." The younger man who had been sitting on the rear corner of the desk rose, flicked an eyebrow at his superior, intercepted and recorded the answering twitch of the grey, bushy head, and walked away into the inner room, closing the door gently after him. "Please, Miss Barber, take this chair. Miss Mather? Be seated, please! And you are Mr. Felse? Yes, we were waiting for you. It was good of you, it was right, to notify us at once."

He might have been sixty, or five years less or more, there was no dating him. He had probably looked much the same for ten years, and wouldn't change for twenty more. Grey at fifty, and still sporting curly, crisp grey hair at eighty-five. No, ninety, he looked remarkably durable. He was not the long, rangy Slovak shape, with great, elegant, shapely bones, but short and sturdy and running to flesh, broad-beamed and broad-breasted, broad-cheeked and wide-eyed, broad-jowled and stubble-chinned, with a bright, beery face. Perhaps of mixed blood, the most inscrutable product in the country, looking now Czech, now Slovak, almost at will. In the high-coloured face the blue, bright, knowing eyes were clear as sapphires, and limpid as spring-water. He was in his shirt-sleeves, his tie comfortably loosened round a bull-neck. Dominic felt better; this was what Mirek Zachar, of fond memory, would have called a

" country uncle." He warned himself vainly that what he felt might be only a false security. He was so tired that it would be dangerous to relax.

" We were grateful for your call. You may rest assured that everything is in hand. Now, naturally, I should like to hear the story directly from you. Please, Mr. Felse! You may speak quite freely. For the moment this is not official." He smiled benevolently into Dominic's tired, drawn face. " You are wondering about my English. It is not so strange. People of my generation here learned English because we had relatives in England or in America. In America especially. We learned English in the hope of going there some day to join them. I was there for five years, before the war, and now I keep up my English from books. My children have forgotten it, my grandchildren do not learn it. They speak excellent Russian, and I am out of date. Times change. It is not matter for regret, only for interest. But I like to use my assets. You need not be afraid that I shall not understand you. Please, speak!"

They were as tongue-tied, after that, as if they had really been confronted with the grim, smooth police official of cold-war fiction, and a good deal more at a loss. Nevertheless, Dominic set to work and ploughed his way doggedly through their agreed story, disliking it more with every word, but making a good job of it.

" Miss Barber and I were out for a walk this evening, after dinner. We ate rather early, I think it must have been about twenty minutes to eight when we went out. We took the road up the valley, and when we got near that small chapel on the hillside there we thought we'd go up and have a look at it."

Lieutenant Ondrejov, a model listener, did not once interrupt, not even with an intelligent and helpful question, but neither did he leave the narration to plod along unencouraged. His round, good-humoured face was encouragement itself, he helped the story along with an occasional sympathetic nod of understanding. They could hardly expect much excitement from him, since he knew already the crucial fact of the murder; but no one could complain that he wasn't responsive. At the end of it he leaned back in his chair with a gusty sigh, and looked from one to another of them thoughtfully, scrubbing at his bristly chin with thick, adroit finger-tips.

" I understand, yes. You went up the valley together, you and Miss Barber?"

" Yes," said Tossa gruffly, lifting the lie from Dominic's shoulders this time. It was the first time Ondrejov had heard that odd, touching little voice of hers, and it made him cock an eye at her with twinkling interest, his grey head on one side.

" And you were together when you heard the shot, and entered the chapel?"

" Yes."

" Tell me, did you know this man at all? The dead man?"

" Not know him, exactly. But we'd seen him once before," said Dominic firmly, " when we were driving through into Slovakia."

" In the hotel at Zilina?" suggested Ondrejov affably.

Four hearts lurched sickeningly towards churning stomachs. He had tugged the ground out from under them like a mat, and the fall, though they sat still and kept their faces obstinately blank, knocked the breath out of them, and the invention with it. He was guessing, with preternatural accuracy, but guessing. He *couldn't* know. They stared polite, patient, uncomprehending enquiry.

" In a hotel somewhere on the way," said Dominic. " We came through so many places, I forget names."

Ondrejov leaned over his desk and wagged a finger at them admonishingly. " Children, children, never try to deceive the old ones. It may be a long time since they were boys, but they have had two refresher courses with their sons and grandsons, and that is much more dangerous. Now, do you want to tell me anything more? Or to think again about what you have already told me?"

Dominic said: " No!" for all of them. What else was

there to say? However disastrously, they were committed now.

"Good! Then let us see if we can contribute something, too." He tilted his chair back, and reached behind him to turn the handle of the inner door. "*Mirku! Pod' sem!*"

Into the room, as fresh and pink and blond as ever, walked Miroslav Zachar, and took up station solidly at his chief's left elbow, confronting with a heightened colour but a placid and purposeful face his four erstwhile friends.

"Mirek," said Ondrejov heartily, slapping the young man resoundingly on the back, "I think you should explain to our young guests exactly what you are doing here. Tell them everything, we have nothing to hide from them."

"I am here," said Mirek simply, "because I discovered the body of Robert Welland this evening. I reported it by telephone from the nearest connected house, which happens to be over the north wall there, in another valley—you would not know the path. Then I waited with the body until the detail came out there, and returned here to report fully in person."

"Perhaps," suggested Ondrejov, "it would help if you explained in full your connection with the affairs of these young people, and how you came to be on the scene tonight. From the beginning!"

"Certainly!" He looked from face to face round the four of them, looked them all fully and firmly in the eyes. Why not? He had nothing to be ashamed of, even if he had been cheated and startled into feeling shame when Tossa kissed him by way of apologising for reservations she should, instead, have respected and re-examined. He had had a job to do, and he knew he was good at it. Dominic, a policeman's son, gave him the ghost of a smile; they were all giving him their fixed and painful attention.

"I was detailed to pick up your party at the frontier, escort you as far as I could, and continue to keep an eye on your movements and your welfare afterwards."

Toddy, hackles erected, demanded: "Why?"

"Why? Naturally Miss Barber, like other visitors, was

obliged to apply for a visa. With the recent events in mind, and certain dimplomatic complications always possible, our police in Bratislava were hardly likely to have left Mr. Terrell's background and circumstances unexamined. They knew that he had married a widow named Barber, with one daughter, now a student at Oxford. The connection was not beyond their ability. They therefore felt that it would be well to keep a protective eye on Miss Barber as long as she remained in this country, for her own good as well as ours. We do not want trouble. There seemed reason to suppose that Miss Barber and her friends were making for the Tatras. I was born here, I used to serve under Lieutenant Ondrejov before I transferred to the plain-clothes branch. As a local man, with good English, and as you see, quite well able to look like a student, I was seconded to this duty."

"Then I suppose this means you've been spying on us ever since you pretended to leave us," said Toddy bitterly.

"I have been carrying out my assignment. Without, I hope, interfering with your enjoyment. This evening I was in cover on the hillside above the chapel, near the crest. There is a place there from which you can cover, with glasses, almost the whole length of the valley. I have often used it. You were within view for perhaps half of your walk, and hidden from me only when among the trees. I saw you come to the chapel."

"And were they together?" murmured Ondrejov innocently.

Into the momentary well of silence, while the four of them held their breath, Mirek dropped his: "No," very gently, but it fell like a stone.

"Did they enter the chapel together?"

"No. Miss Barber came first. It was clear from her manner that she thought she was alone, but I had already seen Mr. Felse carefully following her. She climbed to the rock shelf, and walked straight to the door of the chapel. I had her within sight until the last few yards. The doorway itself was out of my sight. Mr. Felse remained in the shadow of the trees, and did not attempt at first to follow her."

"And then?"

"Then there was a shot. It came perhaps five or six seconds after Miss Barber passed out of my sight and into the chapel. I could not determine from which direction the sound came, it is very difficult in such an enclosed and complex place. It *could* have been fired from outside, even from some distance. But my immediate impression was that it came from within the chapel itself."

Tossa's hands, linked in her lap, tightened convulsively, but she made no sound. It was Toddy who flared in alarm and anger: "That's a lie! You're trying to frighten her! You know it isn't true!"

"Please, Mr. Mather! Go on, Mirek, what next?"

"Mr. Felse dropped to the ground and scrambled across to the doorway. They were in there for several minutes together. I was raking the valley for any signs of movement, but I found nothing. I therefore began to work my way down the slope towards the chapel, but as you know, it is rather a risky field of scree there, one must go cautiously. While I was still well above, I saw Miss Barber dart away from the doorway and run down the path among the trees. After perhaps five more minutes Mr. Felse followed her. It was then beginning to be dusk. He had a fall on the rocks as he ran across the open ground. It was then I saw that Miss Barber had waited for him, just within the trees."

"And by the time you got down there?"

"They were both well away. And when I entered the chapel I found Mr. Welland's body there."

"Mr. Felse stayed behind, perhaps, just long enough to go through the dead man's pockets?" suggested Ondrejov placidly.

Involuntarily Dominic let out an audible gasp of disgust, remembering that the idea had never even occurred to him. And Miroslav smiled.

"I don't suggest he did do so, but the time would have been sufficient, yes."

"And did you hear a second shot, as Mr. Felse says? When he fell?"

"I did not hear one, no. Admittedly I was coming rather quickly down the scree, and I was concentrating on my foot-work, as well as making a considerable noise of my own."

Tossa raised her heavy eyelids just long enough to flash a glance at Dominic, and intercept his startled glance at her. They had heard the scree shifting, and never dreamed of looking up there for a witness.

"One more point," said Ondrejov comfortably, stretching his broad shoulders back until the chair creaked. "The encounter at Zilina. Did it appear to you that Miss Barber was acquainted with Mr. Welland?"

"Yes, quite certainly she was."

"And did she, then, behave naturally when meeting him there?"

"No, she affected not to know him. As I think her friends really did not. But she took occasion to pass a message to him, and he almost certainly passed one back to her."

"Such as this folded scrap of paper, perhaps?"

Ondrejov produced it gently from his pocket, unfolded it with deliberation, and read aloud in his amiable rolling bass: "I shall be at the Riavka hut. Please contact me!" He looked up over Tossa's note with twinkling blue eyes narrowed in an indulgent smile. "If our young and chivalrous friend did go through the victim's pockets, he didn't make a very good job of it, it seems. Zachar has had more practice, of course," he added by way of consolation to Dominic, and folded the paper carefully away again.

"So it seems we have a somewhat changed picture now. You are sure there is nothing you wish to add or alter?" Where would have been the point? All their lies were already demolished, and to think up new ones now would be worse than useless. They were silent, watching him with closed faces and apprehensive eyes. "In that case you must see my predicament. And you should also take into consideration the fact that as yet the cartridge-shell has not been found, and since the bullet is still embedded in the dead man's skull, and only an autopsy can recover it for examination, so far as we know up to now it could as well be from a pistol as a rifle. Couldn't it?"

Tossa was the last to see where he was leading her. She stared from behind these serried facts as through bars, and shook her head helplessly, trying to shake away the sense of nightmare that oppressed her.

" None of us has a gun, or ever had one," said Dominic quickly and quietly. " Certainly Tossa couldn't have had one on her last night. I was following her every step of the way."

" But at a safe distance. And certainly is a large word. A small pistol is not so difficult to conceal."

" She was never out of my sight for more than a few seconds."

" The few seconds when the shot was fired."

" But this is fantastic!" cried Toddy wildly. " For God's sake, how could she cart a gun about with her without my sister seeing it, sooner or later? How could she get it into the country?"

" Oh, come, Mr. Mather! Are you really suggesting our frontier staff are so thorough? Did they even open your cases at Rozvadov?"

Tossa put up her hands wonderingly, and touched her throbbing temples and drawn cheeks as though to satisfy herself that she was still in her own day-to-day flesh, and not astray in a bewildering and terrifying dream.

" But I've never even touched a gun, not once in my life. If you really believe I had one, then where is it now? What did I do with it?" Her voice was so heavy that she could hardly lift the syllables. Like her eyelids, like her heart.

" Ah, that is an open question. The obvious thing to do with it would be to toss it out of the window immediately. But the valley is large enough, and the dusk by then was deep enough, to make it a very open question indeed. So no doubt you will realise, my dear Miss Barber, why I am obliged to keep you, for the present, in custody."

: :   : :

The next ten minutes were confused, noisy and angry. Tossa sat mute and numb in the middle of the storm, too tired to distinguish voices any more, too disoriented to know friend from foe, too deeply aware of having lied, and forced Dominic to lie, to put up any fight for her own liberty. Christine had an arm clasped tightly about her shoulders, and was adding a soprano descant to Toddy's spirited impersonation of an Englishman at bay. Toddy raved about police states, conspiracies and frame-ups, and threatened everything from diplomatic intervention to gunboats. In the heart of her desperate confusion and solitude Tossa remembered inconsequently that Czechoslovakia had no coastline, and laughed, genuinely laughed, but no one noticed except, perhaps, Ondrejov, who noticed everything, whether he acknowledged it or not. He looked like a good-humoured, clever peasant, and he sat here behind his desk manipulating them all. She suspected that he was very much enjoying Toddy. There couldn't be much theatre in Liptovsky Pavol.

"Now, now, my dear boy, I guarantee that Miss Barber shall be well treated, and we'll take every care of her. And since it's too late now for the rest of you to think of going back to Zbojská Dolina to-night, I'll make arrangements for beds for all of you, and we'll call the hut and tell the Martíneks you're staying here."

"That isn't good enough! You know very well that you've no right to detain Miss Barber. As the person in charge of this case, *you* will be held responsible."

Pale with rage, Toddy stood between Tossa and her captors, his nostrils pinched and blue with desperation, as gallant as he was ineffective. Dominic, deep sunk in his own silence and doubt, stared hard at Ondrejov, and wished he could read his mind, but it was impenetrable. Did he really suspect Tossa? Or had he quite another motive for this move? He swung in an agony of indecision between two opinions. The one thing of which he was in no doubt at all was that it was his job to get Tossa out of this. Toddy could make as much fuss and noise as he liked, it wouldn't be done that way. If Ondrejov had been what Toddy claimed he was, he would have laid Toddy flat long before this. And let no one think he couldn't do it single-handed, as old as he was!

" In charge? *I* in *charge* of the case?" Ondrejov's blue, bright eyes widened as guilelessly as a child's. " You think such cases as this are left to the uniformed branch here? No, no, I am waiting at this moment for the plain-clothes people to arrive from Bratislava. I am responsible to them. That is why I am compelled to hold you available, you see, *my* field of action is strictly limited. The men from Scotland Yard," he said, pleased with this flight of fancy, " will be here in a matter of a few hours. You may put your objections and make your statements to them."

" Then at least," said Toddy valiantly, hunted into a corner but still game, " I demand that the British Embassy in Prague shall be contacted at once, and informed that Miss Barber is being held on suspicion."

" The British Embassy," said Ondrejov, dwelling upon the luscious syllables with sensuous pleasure, " has already been informed. As a matter of courtesy, you understand, Mr. Welland being a British national and a member of their staff. They will also be informed that Miss Barber is here, and may be held on suspicion of murder. By to-morrow morning, no doubt, someone will be flying in to take care of her interests, and I can assure you I shall make no objections."

They fell back and studied him afresh in silence, with something of the embarrassment of people who have flung their full weight against an unlatched door and fallen flat on their faces, but with a residue of distrust, too. Did he mean it? It appeared that he did, for he wasn't even troubling to lay any great emphasis on the correctness of his proceedings; but what he intended should follow from them wás another matter. Perhaps he was simply covering himself, and making sure that all the awkward decisions should be left to his superiors, when they came. That was human and credible enough, in any country, in any force.

" When it comes to the point," said Dominic, on the heels of the dubious silence, " Tossa has nothing to be afraid of." He was curiously in doubt, himself, whether he was speaking for her or for Ondrejov. " As soon as the bullet's recovered it will clear her completely. Because it will be a rifle bullet."

" Now that," said Ondrejov, fixing him with a bright and calculating eye, " is a sensible observation. To-morrow," he went on briskly, dropping the pretence of harmlessness as blithely as he would have dropped a cigarette-end, " I suggest you may all prefer to move to the hotel here, and remain near Miss Barber. When you have satisfied yourselves that there are people present to take care of her interests, perhaps *you*, Mr. Felse. . . ." The blue eye dissected him again, with analytical detachment and interest. ". . . will be so good as to drive your van back to Zbojská Dolina to settle the bill and collect your luggage."

He still sounded like a country uncle, but one you wouldn't care to fool with; and there was no mistaking that this was an order.

" It will be interesting," said Ondrejov meditatively, " to see who does turn up to take the responsibility for Miss Barber." He smiled into the inscrutable distances of his own thoughts, which were certainly more devious than his bucolic appearance suggested, and repeated pleasurably: " Very interesting!"

Chapter 8

THE MEN WHO CAME TO THE
RESCUE

The man in charge arrived in Liptovsky Pavol at about four
o'clock in the morning, having preferred to go directly to
the scene of the crime and make his own observations on the
spot, before taking over the office end of affairs from the
local force. He brought with him a very smart police car
from Bratislava, a driver, and two subordinates, which en-
tourage was in itself a more signal recognition of Robert
Welland's V.I.P. status than he had ever received in his
lifetime.

The officer's name was Kriebel, and he looked like an
alert, confident, athletic schoolmaster. He was two steps
above Ondrejov in rank, six inches taller, and twenty-five
years younger, and he weighed up his man in one long,
careful glance, and then enthroned himself casually on a
corner of the desk, and swung his legs. This move, which
established their relationship while keeping it informal, also
deprived Ondrejov of his own favourite chair without putting it into use for his superior officer. To Kriebel a tactful
gesture, it seemed to Ondrejov merely silly. But he was
adroit at handling young men who were ambitious, sensitive
of their rights and advantages in the presence of the old and
stagnating, and considered themselves to be handling him.
This one wouldn't give him much trouble. He had never
wanted to move into the plain-clothes branch himself, and
not only because it would have meant moving from Pavol.
He knew where his talents lay.

He planted himself squarely on his two sturdy legs, and
made his report reasonably fully. The young people? They
were all put to bed long before this, the girl Barber in the
cell downstairs, the others at Pavol's single small hotel. Had

they made formal statements? No, he had preferred to wait for the arrival of the detectives from Bratislava. He contrived to suggest that he had been a little nervous of pressing four English students very far, with the possibility of an international incident obviously hanging over them like a storm-cloud. He outlined the evidence against Tossa, colouring it brightly and then slightly deprecating its brightness, even suggesting that it was not enough of a case to justify holding her. Kriebel, listening and frowning a little, found the tone too patronising on one hand and too timid on the other, and came to the considered conclusion that the girl should be held.

The body of Robert Welland was by then being manhandled from the chapel towards the ambulance that waited for it at the Riavka hut, on its way to Liptovský Mikuláš, where the experts were sleepily and crossly preparing its reception.

"And the other three?" asked Ondrejov, with hunched shoulders and dissenting face. "None of them can possibly have been involved in the actual killing, only the girl Barber had the opportunity. I take it there's no need to interfere with their plans? We can reach them at Zbojská Dolina whenever you want them, there's no particular advantage in keeping them here."

"On the contrary, I think it's essential to have them under our eyes. We'd better fix them up here in the town, and keep them under surveillance, at least until we get the medical and laboratory reports. Then we'll know better what we're handling."

All very well being correct and courteous with foreigners, but Kriebel carried the responsibility, and this was murder.

"As you think," said Ondrejov austerely, with a face so blank that a duller man than Kriebel couldn't have failed to deduce what it was concealing. "Then after you've seen them, I'd better send the young man Felse off with their van to bring their things from the Riavka, and settle them in here at the Slovan."

"I should be glad if you would," said Kriebel, his voice

noticeably thinning as the woodenness of Ondrejov's face thickened.

" Certainly, Comrade Major, whatever you say."

If you want a superior, half your age, to keep things rolling your way, there's nothing like persuading him that the idea was his in the first place, and that you cordially disapprove of it. Ondrejov wasn't going to have the slightest trouble with this one.

" By the way, Comrade Major, I've notified the British Embassy of the girl's situation. Since they're concerned in any case, the victim being one of their own men, I thought it wise to forestall any criticism on that head. I hope that's all right? It won't, of course, affect your handling of the case in the least," he hastened to add, with a nice blend of flattery and malice.

It wouldn't now, at any rate. Ten ambassadors threatening all the professional reprisals in the world couldn't have made Kriebel release his hold of Tossa Barber, after that.

                    : :   : :

It was some hours more before the rescue party began to gather. Even Kriebel had to sleep, after driving some three hundred kilometres from the Slovak capital, and then putting in an hour and a half of intensive work in Zbojská Dolina; consequently the four enforced guests of the establishment were also, by native standards, allowed to lie late, though not, to judge by the look of them when they were finally assembled in the police office, to sleep late.

Only Tossa, once stretched out on the cot in her small, bare room, had collapsed out of the world as though hit on the head with a blackjack; it was her only way of escape from a load temporarily too much for her to carry or comprehend. They dragged her out of her refuge too soon, but at least she had been able to withdraw for a few hours into the utter darkness and indifference of irresponsibility.

She came back to her distorted and frightening world drunken and stunned with sleep, but calm. She was glad, in a way, that they had kept her segregated even from Christine; the load was hers, and sympathy and advice

would only have confused her. As it was, though she hadn't
spent one waking minute thinking about it, she had a very
clear idea of what she had to do. Last night there had
seemed no point in correcting her false story, since Mirek
had effectively established what was false in it; now it
seemed to her essential that she should tell it herself as fully
as she could. There were still things she could not talk
about; but to admit that she had felt unsatisfied about her
stepfather's death, and set out deliberately to investigate it
herself, need not involve the Marrion Institute at all. No
lies this time. Truth and nothing but truth, if not all the
truth. It might not help her out of her mess, but it would
do something to put her right with herself.

"I want to make a statement," she said, when Ondrejov
came to fetch her up to the office.

"So you shall soon, but not to me. And don't be in too
big a hurry." He looked her over with shrewd and thoughtful eyes. "Finish your coffee, there's plenty of time."

She shook her head; it seemed to her an odd attitude.
"The men from Scotland Yard came, then?" she said,
with a pale, brief smile.

"They're not the only arrivals. There are three gentlemen here to get you out of trouble."

"Three?" She was impressed and amused, in a sad and
private way, even very slightly curious, but she didn't care
to ask him questions; in her position it didn't seem to her
that it would be the thing to do. "I don't think they can,"
she said, after a moment's rueful reflection. "Not for a day
or two, anyhow, not until your people have found the
bullet."

"No," agreed Ondrejov smugly. "I don't think they
can."

"Are the others all right? Shall I see them?"

"They're all right, and you'll see them."

They were already in the outer office when he followed
her up the narrow stairs and through the thick brown door.
Swollen-eyed and uneasy after a wakeful night, they sat
silent, waiting to be interviewed, the youngest detective

keeping a cool eye on them from behind the desk. Their
eyes lit at the sight of her, and Dominic came eagerly out
of his chair; but before anything could be asked or
answered the inner door opened, and Kriebel leaned out.

"In here, please, Miss Barber."

She turned one quick glance in Dominic's direction, and
for an instant they stared helplessly at each other. Then she
went on obediently into the inner room, and Ondrejov followed her in and closed the door.

"Miss Barber, my name is Kriebel. I am in charge of
this investigation. Please sit down!"

The chair that had been placed for her was in front of a
large table, and in the full light from the window. Beyond,
the rest of the room seemed dim by comparison, and it was
larger than the shabby little outer office, obstinately and
characteristically preferred by Ondrejov, so that she did not
immediately sort out the strangers from the plain-clothes
men among those present. Her tired but competent mind
could deal with only one thing at a time.

"I should like to make a statement."

That brought the rescuers forward to declare themselves
at once, as if she had sounded an urgent alarm. Three of
them, just as Ondrejov had said, all suddenly revealed as
English the moment they moved and drew her eyes to them.
English with the ludicrous, staggering Englishness which, as
Toddy had rightly observed, is never even detectable at
home. And all of them willing her to silence and delay.

"Miss Barber, I advise you to think carefully about your
position, and do nothing in haste."

"We are here to take care of your interests, Miss
Barber."

The first of them was a middle-aged gentleman of immaculate appearance, smooth-faced, grey-haired, rounded
and agile, with a lawyer's cagey face; the second a long,
loose-limbed young man with a handsome, superior countenance, like a clever horse or a county dowager, and an alert
and impudent eye. The third, who had stayed where he
was and said nothing so far, looked at once the most truly

concerned and the most likely to be effective. He was perhaps even more English than the others, but in a way which looked more at home here, with the fields only a stone's throw away, and the crests of the mountains bright in the distance outside the window. Almost elderly, tall and rather thin, with dark hair silvered at the temples, and a good-looking, well-preserved face that could have belonged equally appropriately to a retired military man or a high civil servant. He had on Bedford cords and a tweed jacket worn into the baggy shapes of comfort, with leather patches at the elbows. the sort of jacket that should be accompanied by a floppy tweed hat to match, preferably with flies stuck round it.

She had never seen any of them before in her life; but of course, they had to take responsibility for all sorts of strays like herself. No wonder the one with the lawyer's face, for all his smooth expression of reassurance, fixed his snapping legal eyes on her as if he detested her. As if it wasn't enough to have an English attaché shot, an English student had to get herself arrested on suspicion of having shot him!

" I beg your pardon, Major Kriebel! Miss Barber should know her rights, she should have time to think, but I realise that you have an urgent duty to do. Have I your permission to speak to her before you question her?"

" By all means! In my presence, of course, at this stage, but, I assure you, quite freely." Kriebel was on impregnable ground, at least pending the medical and ballistic reports; he could afford to be generous. " Miss Barber, these gentlemen are from the British Embassy in Prague. They are here to look after your interests in this unfortunate situation. Please, Counsellor!"

" My name is Charles Freeling," said the lawyer. " I am counsellor to the embassy. And this is Adrian Blagrove, who is assisting us with the preparation of some technical data for translation, in connection with the new trade agreement consultations. I brought him along because he used at one time to work with your late stepfather, and naturally he'd like to assist you if he can. And here," he indicated the man in the tweed jacket, who came forward with a sudden brief, kind smile, rueful and charming, " here is Sir Broughton Phelps, whose name will be known to you, I'm sure. Sir Broughton happened to be on holiday in the White Carpathians, I took the liberty of passing on word to him about you when the news came in."

Yes, that, at least, was a name she knew. So the Director of the Marrion Research Institute " happened " to be on holiday here! And hadn't she heard the other name before, too? Blagrove? Hadn't Robert Welland mentioned him as the new Security Officer? The man who had stepped into Herbert Terrell's shoes? And suddenly he turned up here, " assisting with the preparation of technical data for translation!"

The shock of enlightenment helped to brace her. Here to look after her interests? They were here, and here in desperate haste, to make sure she gave nothing away. That granted, no doubt they'd do their diplomatic best for her.

" Your stepfather was on my staff, my dear." Sir Broughton took her hand, looking down at her with his warm, worried smile. " I shall be only too glad if I can do anything to help you. Freeling was trying to contact me most of the night, it seems. They managed to reach me early this morning at Topolcianky. I've been fishing down in that district." She'd been right about the flies. " I shouldn't worry too much, you know. You haven't done anything you shouldn't, have you? Then it's only a question of telling your story sensibly, and having a little confidence in the authorities."

A beautifully ambiguous reassurance, but she correctly interpreted the warning.

" It was very good of you all," she said dutifully, " to rush to help me like this. I'm afraid you must have spent the night driving."

" Blagrove and I came in to Poprad by air taxi, early this morning," said Freeling. " Sir Broughton drove up from Topolcianky. We were very grateful for such prompt notification of poor Welland's death and your situation,

and for Major Kriebel's courtesy in allowing us to see you
at once. Now, the main thing is that you should think carefully, both about your rights *and your responsibilities*, and
do nothing in haste. No one can demand a statement from
you, you must realise that."

"No one is demanding it," she said. "I want to make it.
I told Lieutenant Ondrejov some things that weren't true,
last night. I want to put them right."

She was saying, it seemed, all the things one should not
say. Everything was topsy-turvy, only her enemies looked
pleased with her, especially Ondrejov, who was beaming so
brightly that his blue eyes were pale as aquamarines in his
brick-red face. The embassy party looked painstakingly
benevolent but inwardly frantic; even Sir Broughton, the
most human of the three, was frowning at her admonishingly.

The pause of glee and consternation was abruptly inter-
rupted by a loud, peremptory voice in the outer room,
speaking unmistakable English. Tossa pricked up her ears
apprehensively, unwilling to trust what they told her. She
looked round for someone who would be quick to understand, and found herself appealing directly to Ondrejov.

"That's somebody else for me, I'm afraid. I know him,
he's—he's a friend of my mother's." How could she say,
with these people still employing the mourning note when
they spoke of Terrell: "He's going to marry my mother."?

Ondrejov got up and went into the outer room, closing
the door between; and presently reappeared with a wooden
face, ushering in before him a large, angry, black-avised
man in an incongruous business suit, who descended upon
Tossa like a perturbed thundercloud.

"For God's sake, girl," demanded Paul Newcombe,
"what have you been up to? Here's your mother phoning
me in Vienna to say she's had word from some chap called
Welland that you're prowling round the regions where
poor old Herbert got killed, and will I please find out what
you're up to, and tell you to stop it. And when I come in
from Austria to the address she says you put on your card

home—and a hell of a job I had finding the place!—I'm told you and your friends have gone, and I'll find you here. *Here, at the police station*! What in the world's been happening?"

Tossa sat shaken and pale. It was going to begin all over again, every one of them worse than the one before. She was going to hate this one as she'd hated Terrell; there was no escape. She looked past the looming shape that was without authority, straight at the two Slovaks who were looking on with such narrow and considering interest.

"Major Kriebel, this is Paul Newcombe. He is not related to me, but as a friend of my mother's I suppose he feels responsible for me. Mr. Newcombe, I was just going to make a statement to Major Kriebel and Lieutenant Ondrejov. It ought to answer all your questions. And with their permission I should still like to make it."

"By all means." Kriebel was moving now partly by guesswork, but not entirely; he had exchanged one rapid glance with Ondrejov, and though nothing appeared to be communicated, something had certainly been understood. "Gentlemen, if you will allow Miss Barber to speak without interruption, you may remain. It is a concession I need not make, but I will make it." Ondrejov's aloof expression and slightly raised brows had said eloquently: "Please yourself, it's your funeral. But *I* wouldn't!" "Comrade Lieutenant, will you take down Miss Barber's voluntary statement?"

: :   : :

"The reason I told some untruths last night, and persuaded Mr. Felse to tell them, too, against his advice, was because I was afraid of becoming more deeply involved if I told the truth. I thought I could give you all the relevant details about Mr. Welland's death, without coming right out and saying that I came here for a special purpose of my own. I persuaded my friends to come, too, and spend the holiday here with me, because my stepfather had died in Zbojská Dolina, and I wasn't satisfied about his death, and wanted to see the place for myself. I met Mr. Welland when he was on leave in London, and we talked about it, and he promised me to look into it himself. But I still wanted to come. I didn't tell him that, and he knew nothing about it until he saw us at Zilina, on our way here. Evidently he didn't approve, since it seems he notified my mother."

She told it exactly as Dominic had suggested yesterday, faithfully admitting Welland's telephone call and her appointment with him, and describing the circumstances of his death. But everything that touched on the Marrion Institute, or national security, or the defection of Karol Alda, still had to be suppressed, and that effectively censored Welland's last cryptic words to her. Had they meant anything, in any case? They stuck in her mind curiously, but their suggestions were too enormous and too vague, she could not trust herself to make a judgment upon them.

There was too much at stake. There sat the Director, listening to her with an anxious and sympathetic face, and willing her to be discreet if it killed her; and the Security Officer, brightly inscrutable, taking her in with cautious approval as she skirted delicately round the establishment that was his charge. She felt it when they began to breathe again. Compared with the secret activities and preoccupations they had to protect, both she and Welland were equally expendable.

Carefully she covered from sight the whole background of the death she most sincerely wanted solved. Right behaviour, she thought sadly, is always a compromise at best.

Ondrejov took down her statement, and presently transcribed it briskly, still in English, on the typewriter in the outer room, and brought it back for her to read and sign. No one tried to prevent her from signing. They were unspeakably relieved by the content of the statement. Her predicament hardly mattered, by comparison; but they gave her to understand, by encouraging glances, that in return for her services they would exert themselves to deliver her.

"I'm only terribly sorry," she said suddenly, her voice a muted cry of protest, "for poor Robert Welland!"

"Of course, of course, so are we all. But I'm sure the affair will soon be cleared up," said Freeling soothingly. "It occurs to me, Major, that as you have no facilities here in Pavol, and it may not be very convenient to move her elsewhere, perhaps you would agree to Miss Barber's being discharged into my custody, pending further enquiries? On the strict understanding, of course, that she shall be made available to you whenever required, and shall not leave the town? I would pledge myself to produce her on demand at any time."

"I hardly think," suggested Sir Broughton Phelps rather drily, "that such a proposition can be entertained if it comes from your people. But as one who had the greatest respect for Miss Barber's stepfather, I should be very glad to abandon my holiday and remain here, if you'll allow *me* to make myself responsible for her? And for her friends, too, though they are not, I believe, in custody?"

Paul Newcombe bristled. "I am representing Mrs. Terrell here, and if Tossa can be released I think it should be into my care."

Ondrejov thumbed through the stapled sheets of Tossa's statement, and hummed a little tune to himself, modal, like the pipe-tunes of Zbojská Dolina. He looked inordinately placid and content, like a fed infant.

"Her friends are quite at liberty, here within Liptovsky Pavol, but I am restricting their movements to the town for the time being. Miss Barber, I regret, must remain my charge. She can be held available to you at any time which is suitable," said Kriebel firmly, "but she is my responsibility. You have heard for yourselves the grounds on which I think it necessary to hold her, and they speak for themselves. Only Miss Barber had the opportunity of committing the murder, so far as we yet know. Of the others, only the boy Felse was also present at the chapel, the others clearly knew nothing about it until afterwards. They will all be invited to record statements, but they will not be held. Miss Barber did have the opportunity, and as you have heard on her own admission, she gave a false account of what happened. She must be held. I have my duty to do."

It was at this moment that Ondrejov chose to look up at his chief and say ingenuously : " Perhaps, Comrade Major, it would be as well if young Felse made his statement next. Then I can start him off to collect their things from the Riavka, while the other two tell us what little they do know. They'll be wanting their clothes and night things."

"Certainly," said Kriebel. " Call him in. And gentlemen, if you wish to remain . . .?"

Now why did he make them that gratuitous offer, she wondered? Not because he owed it to them, not because he felt pressed; on the contrary, he was more at ease every moment. He wanted to see what their response would be, whether they would jump at the chance of staying to make sure that Dominic's account would bear out Tossa's, and frowning him away from any undesirable revelations; and he wanted to observe their reactions if there were indiscretions—and indeed, even if there were none.

Three of them relaxed, cautiously but perceptibly. " That's very considerate of you," said Freeling. " We have a duty to all four of these youngsters, we shall be glad to stay."

Only Paul Newcombe got to his feet, thick and glossy and lowering like a prize bull. " My job is to look after Miss Barber. Do I understand that she must continue in custody?"

" I regret that she must," said Kriebel crisply.

" I would remind you that I've had no opportunity yet to talk to her, and that I'm here at her mother's request. May I have a quarter of an hour with her, at least?"

The glance that flickered back and forth between Ondrejov and his superior was almost too rapid to be visible, but Tossa caught it.

" If you go down with her now, you may have a short interview with her, by all means."

Paul jumped at it, was even surprised into expressions of appreciation; they were being almost excessively correct. Tossa wondered about these concessions herself, until she had been led helplessly past the anxious three fidgeting in the outer room, and down the stairs to her cell. Then she understood. The plain-clothes escort who opened the door for them and followed them in was Miroslav Zachar; if Paul had anything of interest to say to her, it certainly wasn't going to be missed.

Ondrejov, ushering Dominic into the inner office, smiled fatly to himself, and sharpened his pencil with a leisurely, enjoying deliberation.

: :   : :

The twins, frayed into nervous silence, were admitted together into the inner room, and Dominic went down the stairs with Ondrejov's hand on his shoulder. Every step seemed to him to be on eggs; or else there was a slack rope under him. He didn't even know whether he'd said the right things, telling half the truth like that, suppressing the other half, with one eye cocked on the anxious, dignified, admonitory English faces, and the other on this gross, earthy, ordinary soul who tramped solidly at his heels. He hadn't even known who they were, those three hanging on his words. They couldn't all be from the embassy, could they?

Mirek had made it necessary to tell the truth about the actual circumstances of Welland's death, to admit that Tossa had gone there to meet him, and had expected him to have something to tell her about her stepfather's accident. As for the rest, he had objected to answering for anything that wasn't known to him personally; hearsay evidence wasn't good in English law, anyhow.

The van was standing in front of the Hotel Slovan, a small, decrepit, gabled house, its portal withdrawn under the arcade of the square.

" Drive carefully," said Ondrejov at his shoulder. " You know the road?"

" I drove here. I know the road."

"You'd do well to eat your dinner there, it'll be time. And on the way back, *drive briskly*. Understand? Don't stop for anything or anyone, keep going, and keep a good pace. Your friends will be waiting for you," said Ondrejov soothingly. "Don't worry about them, they'll be all right. Miss Barber, too. I'll take care of her."

"Who was the other one?" Dominic asked abruptly. "The one who went off with Tossa?"

"You don't know? A Mr. Newcombe. It seems he feels himself to be in the place of a father. I assume her mother is thinking of marrying him."

"Oh! I see!" His tone indicated that he did not see very clearly. He climbed into the driving seat of the van, and inserted the key. The engine quivered into life. "She isn't alone, is she?" he asked, his mind suddenly very clear and very calm. "She won't be alone?"

"She won't be alone at all. I have two daughters, my boy. I have a grand-daughter. You can be easy."

The miracle was that he instantly felt easy. He started the van moving. It rolled across the cobbles of the square, towards the neatly patterned width of roadway, sailed decorously into it, and vanished between the step-gabled façades at the far end.

Mirek Zachar materialised at Ondrejov's elbow, large and placid from the shadow of the arcades, buckling his crash-helmet under his chin.

"This man Newcombe's booked in here, at the Slovan. All right, I can keep the kid in sight, don't worry. I know these roads better than he does. You'll be at the bend by Král's, in case?"

"Or someone else will. We'll be keeping constant watch there. If anything goes wrong, if there's anything even questionable, telephone."

"Surely!" said Mirek, and straddled his Jawa and kicked it into life before it was out of the arcade.

"If you lose him," threatened Ondrejov, raising his voice peremptorily above the din, "I'll have your hide for a jacket!"

Chapter 9

THE MAN WHO REAPPEARED

Now that he was on his own he could think; he had a lot of thinking to do, and seven miles of driving to help him to do it. The one thing he knew for certain was that everything rested on him. They might come running from all directions to Tossa's aid; the responsibility for her, nevertheless, belonged simply to herself and Dominic, no one else. And Tossa was a prisoner, and immobilised; so there was no one left but Dominic.

Unless, perhaps Ondrejov . . . ? His actions were apparently orthodox, but there was something about him that continually indicated the possibility of deception, as though he enjoyed making all the signposts point the opposite way. But the trouble was that one couldn't be sure, and there wasn't time to wait and watch developments. So that left the answer the same as before; it was up to Dominic.

The details of Welland's murder had to make sense every murder must make sense. A distorted sense sometimes, where a distorted mind is involved, but Dominic had a feeling that there was nothing in the least deranged in this killing. Therefore, if he had all the facts at his disposal, he ought to be able to work it out; but since he had not all the facts, he must be prepared to fill in some of the gaps with intelligent speculation.

Start with something positive : someone was prepared to kill in order to ensure that people from Karol Alda's English past should not contact him. First Terrell, then Welland, as soon as they got too near to finding Alda, and both of them within the same small valley. Therefore Alda was there to be found, either in person, or in such strong indications as could not fail to lead directly to him elsewhere. But because of the urgency which apparently had attached to removing the hunters at short notice, it seemed to Dominic more likely that the man himself was there. Not certain, but for present purposes a reasonable assumption.

Was it therefore necessarily true that Alda himself had done the killing? He was wary of thinking so; if he and his work were now vitally important to this country, and had to be kept secret, far more likely that the necessary killing would be undertaken by professionals experienced in the art, leaving the genius to work undisturbed. That was assuming that this was really national business, of course. If it was a personal murder with a personal motive behind it, then Alda was, presumably, taking care of his own privacy.

In either case, if it was as vital as all that, the next move was already implied. Because whoever had shot Welland had also got in a second shot at Dominic on that occasion. He knew, all too well, that there had been one witness there, probably he knew there had been two, and who they were. He could not know whether Welland had had time to give up his secrets to them before he died, and he could not afford to take risks. They were both dangerous to him, and due for removal. If he knew enough, Tossa would be his chosen target. But Tossa was safely out of circulation and out of his reach. And who had put her there? Ondrejov, that inscrutable, innocent countryman.

The striped fields under the hills danced by outside the windows of the van, and he was back at the enigma of Ondrejov once again. Was Tossa really being held because he—or his superior, or both—suspected her? Or because, like a true policeman, he refused to let her run free and be used for bait?

Either way, that left Dominic Felse next in line; and Dominic Felse was not out of circulation; he was here in the van, driving along a mountain road, alone.

Was there anything else positive to go on? Too much speculation was only beginning to confuse the issue. Yes, there remained, if nothing else, the few words Robert Welland had left behind him in dying. Tossa had reported them as: " But he couldn't have known—nobody else knew!" And then, furiously: " Impossible!" Welland had almost certainly been convinced that Alda had killed Terrell. Therefore Alda must be the " he " who couldn't have known, presumably, that Welland had actually located him. How, then, could he have acted on the knowledge? And then: " Impossible!" What was impossible in Welland's eyes? Certainly not that Alda should attempt to kill him; that was something he could, by his own theory, have expected.

He had reached the curve of the road where the rutted track turned off to the right, into Zbojská Dolina. The van rounded the bend, and began to climb. Another mile, and the low roof and deep eaves of the Riavka hut budded suddenly like a mushroom out of the meadow grass, with the bluish, fragrant darkness of the firs behind.

Somehow he had arrived at a totally unexpected conclusion, and no matter how much he walked round it and looked for other ways, they all brought him back to this one need. In the tangle of secrecy, suspicion and subtlety they had all been hunting for one person, but without ever speaking his name, ever asking after him, ever pausing to consider that he might not even know they wanted him. Never had it occurred to them that he might not be hiding or avoiding them at all, but only quite oblivious of them, because they were too sure of their sophistication to ask their way to him, and let him speak for himself. It is the only thing the twentieth-century spy must not do, go straight towards his objective. But how if this wasn't a real-life spy story at all, but something at once simpler and deeper?

He still didn't know what he was going to do when he brought the van lumbering to a standstill on the stony level outside the Riavka gate. All he was sure about was that there was no time left for going roundabout. The police could hardly hold Tossa, once the ballistics report proved

they had a rifle to hunt for, and how long would that be?
Could he rely on more than this one day?

He needed immediate action; he needed an open, honest
solution, however inconvenient to however many people,
because only such a solution could deliver Tossa. Not
simply free her from custody, but deliver her from her own
complex captivities, and make her look forward into the
world with the same wonder and clarity he had seen in her
eyes just once, when she had believed she might be going
to die.

What he needed, and needed desperately, was Karol
Alda.

::   ::

The Martíneks were a little constrained, but genuinely
kind. Even Ivo came down from the pastures to hazard his
few halting words of English. Dana helped by packing the
girls' things, and her brother loaded the van, while Dominic
ate the lunch Mrs. Martínek laid for him on the corner
table in the bar. He paid the bill, rather shyly contriving
to avoid picking up the change; and Dana, ambassador for
the family, went out to the doorstep with him to say good-
bye. But the slight constraint was still there, and her words
were still carefully chosen. He couldn't blame her. Nobody,
in any country, wants to be mixed up with crime and possible treason. If he asked her, now, the questions that
should have been asked at the beginning, she would not
answer them.

He took the van far enough down the track to be out of
sight, and then drove it aside at a relatively level spot, and
parked it among the trees, where it would not be immediately noticed. Then, making a detour in cover about
the Riavka clearing, he set out to climb the valley.

It was just past one o'clock, fine and clear and warm,
with a fresh breeze that made walking pleasant. There was
no one stirring but himself; Zbojská Dolina was not high
enough to be fashionable, and at midday the herdsmen were
eating and sleeping by turns, somewhere out of sight. It
occurred to him, when he came to the defile where the

chapel loomed on its shelf of limestone, that he was still wearing the dark-red sweater he had worn the previous evening, and that it was as conspicuous at noon against the greens of grass and bushes, as it had been unobtrusive in the dusk, where all dark things were parts of the general darkness. There might well be policemen working here, combing the tumbled, bushy ground below the shelf, for the non-existent pistol Tossa might conceivably have had about her and tossed through the window after the murder. But it was too late to do anything about it now. He drew aside into the trees wherever he could; but he saw no one, and heard nothing but the chirring of crickets and the vibration of the conifers in the breeze.

He came into the upper bowl of the valley, where the huts clustered at the edge of the brilliant bog grass. They were silent, too. On such a warm and settled afternoon everyone would be up in the high pastures, drowsing among the folds of crest-country where an army could scatter and vanish. It wasn't easy to distinguish sheep here, they fused with the pale, stony colours and sometimes refused to be detected even in motion. Only the chestnut goats burned like tiny, active jewels in the bleached grass.

He was ranging slowly up the slope, in an easy spiral, when he saw them dancing daintily along the contour path high above him, towards the outcrop rocks that contained the northern col. Behind him and a little below him lay the isolated hut, the highest in the valley; before him was the corrugated, sidelong fall of grass, and then the long grey scar of the rock chute that poured the debris of the heights down to the talus on the ledge. He stood on a level with the upper face of the talus, and not fifty yards from where its first spilled stones welled over into the grass and peppered the slope. It didn't look so terrible from here, or so steep; it looked almost like a very rough and irregular path, a replica of the one above, but built up ten feet high with stones. The sheep-path on which he stood led vaguely up to it, and there turned to the right, and climbed the staircase of terraced tracks, tread by tread.

And high above him, mincing delicately towards the col, the dark-red goats made a dotted line of colour, with the tall brigand-figure of their herd striding at the head of the line. This time there was no frieze cloak, and no hat glittering with a band of fine chains. But there were the cream felt trousers, the wide-sleeved white shirt, the dappling of embroideries, the length and looseness of that mysterious body, the only one in Zbojská Dolina he had not seen at close quarters. The only one!

Dominic cupped his hands about his mouth, and sent a high, yodelling shout up towards the crests. The goats bounded on, unperturbed. The man halted, two full seconds later, as though the sound had only just risen to him, and looked at leisure about the valley below him. Dominic knew the moment when he was seen. He was the only alien creature there to be found, and the practised eye could not choose but find him. He waved an arm, and an arm was waved casually in return, before the remote figure turned to climb higher.

He would go; there was nothing to keep him, and only fifty yards or so to climb before he slipped through the pass and was lost. And even if pursued, would he be found again? He had time to vanish utterly before Dominic could reach the crests.

There was no moment when he consciously chose what he would do. All he was aware of was of doing it, without hesitation and without argument. Afterwards he did remember feeling glad, after all, about the dark-red sweater that made him a land-mark; and he recalled a sort of logical thought-process which he had probably adopted after the event, to rationalise his actions. If he could not reach the stranger in time, then the stranger must be drawn back to him. Mountain men are for ever suspicious of the folly of visitors, and their unbelievable innocence in dangerous places. It is their instinct to pull novices out of trouble. They can no more ignore the challenge than a fireman can pass by a fire.

He was on the stony edges of the talus almost before he realised it himself; straight ahead, from the dead end of the contour path that turned and climbed here sensibly on solid ground, straight on to the giant's causeway of boulders. And it was too late to yodel again now, and too late to look up and make sure that he was observed. It was suddenly a wonderfully simple world, and there was only one enemy, and only one issue, whether he survived or died.

If he had really been an innocent, it would have been an easy thing to start on that journey; but if he had been an innocent he would never have done it, because he would not have known that it could serve his purpose. And because he was no raw novice, he began to suffer even before the first solid boulder shivered like jelly under his foot, and brought him up in tense balance, his breath held, his arms spread for stability. It was even more difficult because he had to look sure of himself until he had gone far enough to drag the goat-herd down from his heights. If he looked a fraud, who would bother to come to his rescue, even when he really needed it?

He was still poised, waiting to take the next step, when he heard the long, peremptory shout above him, and his heart turned over and melted in crazy gratitude. He dared not look up. Sweat broke on his body as he raised one arm and waved briefly and precariously in acknowledgment, like a cheerful fool completely misunderstanding the warning. He had to go on. How long would it take the herdsman to drop down the slope to him? How much farther must he go on this quaking, lurching, insecure pathway, that led nowhere except, in a ruinous fall, down to the bottom of the bowl?

He couldn't look up, and he couldn't look down. He had read Norman Douglas, too; he wanted to take his grim advice, and drop sensibly on to all fours, to lower his centre of gravity as far as possible, and avoid the shifts of weight that would roll the first stone onward over the ledge, and set the whole appalling mass in motion. There wouldn't be much left to identify, if he went overboard with this lot. A coffee-grinder couldn't do a better job on the bean that slid down into its teeth, than these stones would do on his body.

And now he couldn't look round, either. Absolute balance was everything. One more step, short and steady, sliding the weight gradually from foot to foot, eyes fixed ahead. He felt like a beach-spider scuttling over a quicksand, but in slow-motion; his sense of proportion was suddenly invaded by the monstrous illusion that every honed rock under his foot was a polished grain of sand slithering away and sucking him under. The quiver of insecurity was everywhere, under him, round him, in the air that embraced him. The temptation to lean inward and clutch at the rock face on his right hand was almost irresistible, but he knew he must not do it. That was the quickest way to urge the first stone gently outwards, and loose the avalanche, himself one grain among the many, and the most vulnerable. The grained grey rock leaned to him invitingly. He drew his hand back fastidiously, steadied his breath, and felt with an outstretched toe for the next precarious and shuddering plane on which he could rest.

It accepted his weight perfidiously, and then at the last moment it lurched, and almost brought him down. He swayed and stared, afraid to close his eyes, fighting for balance, streaming with sweat in a sudden flood that scalded his eyebrows and eyelids, and burned bitterly on his lips. His supporting foot slipped, the stone under it rolled with agonising slowness between its fellows, and ponderously found a new equilibrium. He was down on hands and knees, quivering, toppling, wrestling with the air within him and without, fighting to balance his terrified flesh with the poised wings of his desperately calm mind. Under his spread, cautious fingers the stone felt like a ploughed field shaken by earthquake. Slowly, slowly the convulsions settled. He hung still, intact, amazed, running with sweat.

Through the thunder of blood in his ears, he heard a voice behind him saying very clearly and coolly: "Don't be startled! Keep quite still. I'm here close behind you."

And indeed the voice was close, steady and sourceless, like voices heard in delirium; and like those voices, it did not startle him, it was strangely acceptable, almost familiar; even the fact that it spoke in unaccented English did not strike him as surprising. The only thing he wondered about then was time. How long could he have been kneeling here sick and blind, fighting for his nerve and his balance, if the stranger had had time to drop down the slope to him and follow him out on to this vibrating man-trap?

"Don't move until I tell you."

A hand, long, large-jointed and muscular, came steadily sliding past his shoulder, and closed over his right hand, holding it down hard against the stone. The hand's invisible fellow settled bracingly under his right arm-pit.

"Now! Turn inward towards the slope. Gently! I've got your weight."

The hands holding him felt like the only stable things in the universe. He trusted them, and turned about the pivot of his own anchored arm. He could see nothing but the close, grained surfaces of rock, and the light on the side of him where the fall was; but now it had changed to his right side. When he had blinked away the sweat that stung his eyes, the range of his vision took in also the hand that gripped his own, a muscular, naked forearm, the edge of a wide linen sleeve, and a knee, cased in cream-coloured felt, drawing back slowly to a new position.

"All right?" asked the voice.

"Yes. I'm all right."

"Keep still, then. I'm going to turn ahead of you. No, keep down!"

The hands withdrew from him. He drew breath cautiously, and through the interstices of his human and commanding terror intimations of reason and will came floating back to him.

"Good! Now follow me closely. I'll go slowly. Hold by my ankle as you move up after me."

"I'm all right. I'll follow."

But sometimes he accepted the offer, all the same, closing

his fingers firmly on the lean ankle above the laced sheepskin shoe, partly for the comfort of another human being's solidity and nearness, even more with a sort of detached elation, because he had risked his life to draw this man down within his reach, and here he was now in the flesh, under his hand.

The way back seemed longer than the way out. They moved by careful inches, spreading their weight low and delicately, like cats. The sun was burning on the exposed nape of Dominic's neck, a new and almost grateful discomfort; the stones were warm under his palms, warm and shaking like live flesh, searing his skinned finger-tips. He felt for the places that had held firm under his guide, gripped the heel of the soft shoe, and crawled doggedly on; until suddenly the shoe was drawn out of his grasp, and set its sole to the ground, and there were a few blades of bleached, seeding grass that fluttered beside the arched foot.

Dominic stared at them, and for a moment could not realise what they were doing there. A hand reached down to lift him by the arm. His companion was on his feet, on the pale, terraced hillside at the end of the talus. They were out of it, and they were alive. Dominic put foot to ground eagerly, and the ground held steady under him; now it was his knees that gave way and all but let him fall.

He could hardly stand. But for the arm that encircled him and hoisted him down the slope, he would have had to sit down in the grass and wait helplessly until the shock and reaction passed. Shamed and dismayed, he let himself be hustled into the highest hut, and dumped without ceremony on the camp-bed that stood in one corner of the single room. He sat with his head in his hands, drawing in deep, steadying breaths, his eyes closed.

A hand tapped him smartly on the shoulder, and he opened his eyes to find a glass being dangled in front of him.

" Here, put this down."

The voice had abandoned its cool, unstartling detachment; it was peremptory, warm and formidably angry.

Dominic took the glass meekly; he didn't know what was in it, but it was fiery and bitter, and burned into all the corners of him with a salutary shock. Everything shook into place again, sun and shadow and forms and thoughts. He realised for the first time the full implications of what he'd done. Apart from risking his life in that perilous passage, he had presented himself as a sitting duck for anyone who wanted to wipe him out. What could he have done in his own defence, quaking out there on a rolling heap of marbles, without even a hand free to throw stones, much less the possibility of running for cover? If he had miscalculated about this man in front of him, he would have been dead by now, and buried, and probably beyond identification if ever they recovered what was left of him.

But he hadn't miscalculated. He was here, alive; and this man had brought him here.

He looked up over the empty glass, the drink stinging his throat and eyes, and for the first time gave all his attention to his rescuer. He found himself looking up into a frowning face, broad across eyes and brow, lean of cheek and long of chin, with a scimitar of a nose, and a long, sceptical mouth. Light brown hair arched high at the temples, duplicating the line of his brows; and the deep eyes beneath stared hard at Dominic, and not precisely indulgently, or with any great liking.

" And now perhaps you'll tell me," he said grimly, " what the devil you thought you were doing, out there?"

" I was looking for you, Mr. Alda," said Dominic. " And I've found you."

Chapter 10

THE MAN IN AMBUSH

There was a moment of silence, blank and profound, while they stared at each other. Anger left the formidable, self-sufficient face, and something of wonder, interest and speculation came into it, but nothing at all of either understanding or disquiet.

"You know my name, it seems. Should I know yours?"

"It's Dominic Felse. But no, you won't know it. I'm English."

"That I'd already gathered," said Alda drily. "Only an Englishman, and I should guess a Londoner, would go striding out on treacherous places with quite such aplomb. Do you realise now that you did your best to kill yourself? Or are you completely a fool?"

The *becherovka* had begun to burn in Dominic's cheeks. "I'm not from London. I'm a countryman, almost a hillman. I knew what I was doing." He was angry with himself the minute he'd said it; it sounded like a child's pique, though he had intended something quite different and very much more respectable. "I've climbed quite a bit," he said, almost apologetically. "I know the sort of places where one shouldn't go."

"Then you *are* completely a fool! Or else," he said, narrowing his deep-set eyes intently, "you wanted me very badly. Perhaps you'd better tell me why."

"You *are* Karol Alda?" He knew it, but he wanted it said.

"They call me Karol Veselsky here. But yes, I am Karol Alda. Karol Alda or Charles Alder, whichever you prefer. And what do you want with him?"

"I've got a friend who's in trouble, and I want your help. It concerns you. But it's quite a story."

"You'd better tell me."

And Dominic sat with his hands gripped tightly together between his knees, and told him, almost in a breath. He was not afraid of not being understood. And now he was no longer afraid of any kind of evasion.

"There are four of us here together, I daresay you've seen us around. One of the girls is Tossa Barber, and her stepfather was a man named Terrell, who was killed here in this valley, about three weeks ago. It isn't that she was fond of him, or anything, but she felt bound to him, and she wasn't satisfied about his death, that's why she got us to come here. She wanted to find out for herself. And what she found out was that *you* were somewhere here, and he'd picked up your trail and was looking for you. Tossa felt it might have been murder. But the Slovak police had closed the case and lost all interest in it."

"Perhaps," said Alda, eyeing him levelly, "because for them there was no mystery about his death."

"You mean they *know* how he died?"

"They know exactly how he died."

"How?" asked Dominic, moistening dry lips. "I mean, how do they *know*?"

"They know because I told them. I reported his death."

"*You reported it?* I thought the Martíneks. . . . They called out the mountain rescue people. . . ." He broke off there, remembering Dana's account of that night search. The Martíneks had notified the mountain rescue service, and then gone out to hunt for their missing guest, but the police had been first on the scene. Because the police, it seemed, had known exactly where to go. "Would you mind telling me about it? This isn't curiosity, it's terribly important."

"It's very simple. I was on my way home by the high-level path that crosses the open rock there. Since you came to investigate his death, I take it you've looked at the place. I wasn't thinking of Terrell. I haven't thought about him for five years at least, I've had other things to think about. I had no idea he was within seven hundred miles of me.

And at the blind point in the path I met him, face to face."
He caught the brief, fearful gleam of Dominic's eyes, the
one returning instant of doubt, and smiled wryly. "No, I
didn't touch him. I had no time for anything beyond
recognising him. Because he'd recognised me, and his reactions were the quicker and the deadlier. He shrank back
from me. Jumped back would be nearer the truth. And
he went over the edge. When I climbed down to him—
it takes ten minutes or so from there—he was already dead.
Well, my own telephone at home was as near as any other,
so I went on there, and called in the police from Pavol.
There was never any mystery for them about his death,
except perhaps the mystery of what he was doing there at
all, in the dusk alone."

"But do they know," asked Dominic pointblank, "about
the connection there was between you before? Did you tell
them he was the man who was put on your case when you
left England?"

Alda's eyebrows rose. "You're very well-informed, I see.
I told them I had known him and worked in the same
institute with him. That was necessary, they wanted him
identified, of course. But as for the rest . . . why bother?
It seemed to me irrelevant. I could and did tell them exactly
how he fell to his death, and they didn't question my
word. I didn't think our past connection had anything more
to say in the matter. The man was dead. I took it for
granted, then, that our meeting like that was pure chance."

"It wasn't! He was looking for you, trying to find out
what you were doing here, what you were working on.
He'd found a piece of scrap paper, music paper, with your
handwriting on it, and that brought him here to Zbojská
Dolina, searching for you. I suppose it would have been
another feather in his cap if he'd been able to bring home
word of something sensational."

He had got so far when he saw that Alda was leaning
back against the wall in a convulsion of silent laughter. He
sat staring, confounded.

"Forgive me! But how baffled he'd have been if he had

found out what I'm working on! Do you know what it is? Do you know why my privacy was left largely undisturbed, why things were arranged so that I did not have to come into the limelight with my story? Because of my vitally important work! Because I am at work on an opera about Comenius! How many sinister codes he'd have read into every note! Especially into the evangelical psalms! That was his profession, and his occupational hazard. It seems he died of it."

Every word rang true. Dominic believed him all the more readily because there was no attempt to convince; belief was taken for granted, as between honest men who recognise each other on sight. But he still did not understand.

"But *why* did he fall? Even if he was startled, even if the dusk was coming on, *why*? He was used to mountains, he climbed the big stuff. Why did he jump back like that? Did he expect you to attack him?"

"Possibly, though nothing was farther from my mind. If only he'd known how little ill-will I bore him, how little I thought of him at all! But more probably he suffered a reflex of conscience, a superstitious recoil. Coming face to face quite inescapably, as he did," said Alda softly, "with a man he had, by his own standards and in his own way, murdered."

: :   : :

Alda lifted the empty glass from Dominic's clenched fingers, and went and refilled it at the rough cupboard on the wall. "Here, it won't hurt you. You still look as if you need it. How much do you know about myself and Terrell and the Marrion Institute? And how did you get to know? Security must be as tight as ever there."

"Tossa had it from a man named Welland, some sort of secretary at the embassy in Prague, who knew Terrell as a good climber, and didn't believe his death could be an accident. He began poking into the past, and he . . . well, he found . . ."

"He found me. Quite! A Slovak, an enemy, a possible murderer. A defecting physicist-cum-mathematician on highly secret work. A little hackneyed now, perhaps, but to him convincing, I'm sure. Do you need to know the rest of it? How much do you know?"

Dominic told him, and blushed feverishly over the telling. It was like recapitulating the plot of a sausage-machine thriller; in this clear air he marvelled that anyone should be able to view motives and actions in such crude and unlikely ways.

"Yes, I think you do need to know everything. After your recent effort," he said tolerantly, "I think you've earned it. When I went off into Savoy for my leave, to consider whether or not I should resign, I went up alone into the highest routes I could manage, and kept in touch with no one, either at home or locally. I was trying to wear myself out, body and mind, in the hope of a revelation. And just at the end of my time I was cut off in a solitary refuge in Dauphiné by bad weather and a slight injury, and kept there for a fortnight. The place was well stocked, and I was glad of the extension. But when I got down into Briançon at last, with a fortnight's beard, burned dark brown, and much thinner than when I went up, I found out from the first English paper I bought that the hysteria of the times had turned me into a fugitive and a traitor. The main points of Terrell's dossier on me were already in print. They hadn't given me even two weeks' grace."

"You mean," demanded Dominic, the glass shaking in his hand, "you never ran away at all?"

"Never until then, certainly. After that you might say I walked away. The hue and cry was out after me as I sat reading the catalogue of my offences in the middle of it. All I did was to accept the omen. No, I didn't run, I walked to the nearest exit. It was a work of art, that dossier. No absolute lies, you understand, only double truths. Maybe it was only the work of a suggestible, ambitious mind bent on rising in his profession, and able to convince himself in the process. Maybe it was coldly and deliberately constructed, for the same personal reasons. I gather he got the Security Office on the strength of the job he did on me. He was a junior in the secretariat when I knew him. All I know is, when we ran headlong into each other he sprang back from me, and went over the edge. How do I know what he saw, and what do I care? Why go further into it now?

" I could have come back, of course, but it would have been to a shower of mud, and a hard fight ahead of me to clear my name. The times were against me. But that wasn't why I walked away. It was disgust I felt, not fear. And something else, too. A sense that a gate had opened before me for a purpose, and I mustn't hesitate to pass through it. So I simply turned, without haste, and walked away again into the blue."

Dominic's teeth chattered faintly against the rim of the glass. " But you must know that you left people in England convinced that you'd changed sides in the cold war. Even your coming back here would be interpreted as backing up that view."

" Boy, I was born here. The old lady who has the farm just over the col is my grandmother. Her home is my home. I became English at fifteen because my parents became English, at a time when I was a minor, and went along naturally with them. Don't misunderstand me, I have nothing against being English. I have simply recognised the fact that in spite of the filling in of papers, I am *not* English. The process is more complex than that. I took my time over the decision, but in the end I came home."

" But you did bring your gifts with you. To be used here."

" Gifts are to be used wherever one goes. But what gifts? That attack on me was an oracle and an opportunity. For years I'd worked earnestly in government service, trying to keep my belief in the professed ideals of government, against all the evidence, forcing myself into the mould of a life for which I was never intended. It took that crisis to make me realise I'd been using my energy in the way least suitable for me, and least effective. Every man must use his own tools for the re-shaping of the world. I've gone back to mine. Music, tranquillity, human affection, human dignity—they can all be used to state the political truths I believe in. Putting aside, of course, the narrower meaning of 'political'. I came home and asked them to take me back as what I am first and foremost, a composer. And they accepted me as a Slovak again on my own terms. I chose to take my grandmother's name, which is Veselsky, simply because I didn't want to be an international sensation or a bone of contention, in Czechoslovakia or England or anywhere else. I refuse to be used as ammunition against either of my two countries, and I need privacy and peace in which to work. They must have thought them reasonable requests—they've been almost too religiously respected."

"Then you're giving *all* your time to music?" asked Dominic doubtfully.

"You think all my time is too much? This pastoral life is only part of the picture. For composition I find it ideal here in the mountains, but there are other aspects of my life, too. I give occasional piano recitals, I do a great deal of conducting. Oh, I assure you all my time is hardly enough."

"No—I suppose not. But in England," ventured Dominic hesitantly, "you had other work as well, this work with aircraft design, and all that. And that was important, too. Tossa said Welland told her you could have been Director of the Marrion. Don't you miss all that? Don't you ever want to get into it again here?" He had not quite the hardihood to add : "And if you don't, why did you bring your notebooks with you?"

Alda smiled. "I won't say it gave me no satisfaction. I may even take it up again some day, if I do it will be in a very different way. Meantime, with only one life to spend, I'm making sure of the first essential first. Nothing is going to elbow out music a second time. But I keep in touch," he said, meeting Dominic's absorbed stare with faintly indulgent good-humour. "I have a friend in America who keeps me supplied with technical magazines. If I ever do decide to get back into the field I shan't be starting under any great handicap. Not that I think it likely," he admitted tranquilly. "If ever I thought myself indispensable, I've been cured of that. At least one of my undeveloped ideas went into commercial production this spring with a French company—and to better effect than if I'd worked it out for the Institute. What they'd have kept it for I daren't imagine. Prunières have incorporated it in a light helicopter for crop-spraying in tropical countries. No secrets, reasonably cheap production, and a sensible use. They're welcome to the profit. I'm content. No doubt somebody or other will happen on all the other ideas, too, given a few years. Simultaneous discovery in music is less likely. I'll stick to music."

"Then, of course," conceded Dominic, "I suppose it wouldn't be liable to occur to you that Terrell might have been prowling round to spy on your work. And you couldn't guess—how could you?—that there was likely to be another death."

"Another death?" Alda looked up sharply. "I've heard nothing about a death. Surely the police would have contacted me?"

"They haven't had much time, it only happened last night. And then, the Terrell case would be closed for them, and they only knew the half of it, they wouldn't connect this with you. And we weren't as helpful as we might have been, because we didn't know . . . we thought that you . . ."

"That I'd killed Terrell, and might well kill someone else? Yes, I see your point. If you've given up that idea now," he said grimly, " you'd better tell me just what's happened."

Dominic told him the story of Welland's death, and all that had followed it. Alda had risen, and was pacing restlessly and silently across the patterns of sunlight and shadow in the window of the hut, which faced down the valley, away from the doorway and the smooth grey scar of rock.

"So your friend is being held on suspicion? And you came to look for me! As a valuable witness, or as the murderer?"

"How could I know which, then? I hadn't met you or spoken to you, all we knew was the Terrell version. Didn't it seem the obvious thing to think at first, that you were picking them off when they got too close? We'd seen you up on the skyline there with the goats, we saw you carried a rifle. . . ."

"A *rifle*?" Alda whirled on him with a face of blank, disdainful astonishment. "*I* carry a *rifle*? I don't think I've ever even had one in my hands. You're dreaming."

"But I did see you with it, up on the crests," protested Dominic, shaken. "A great long stock sticking up over your shoulder, and the barrel . . ."

He broke off, hopelessly confounded. Alda had flattened his wide shoulders against the shadowy wall of the hut beside the window, and was laughing his heart out.

"I don't understand." Dominic was on his feet, his face burning, a little from the conviction that he had somehow made himself foolish, but much more from the *becherovka*. "In any case I'd really stopped believing it was you doing the shooting, before I came up here looking for you, but I know what I saw. . . ."

"But you don't! That's exactly what you don't know, but *I* do, now. This . . . this is what you saw." He crossed the dim room in three vehement strides to the corner behind the iron stove, cluttered with tools, and draped with the black felt cloak he had worn in the storm, and disentangled from behind its veiling folds a long object, which he brought forward into the light from the window, and held upright for inspection, laughing still.

It was within three inches as tall as Alda himself, and about as thick as a child's wrist, a tube of pale wood polished by age and handling. To the back of it, at the upper end, was secured by closely plaited hemp cords a narrower pipe about two feet long, a small round mouthpiece jutting from the back of it at the lower end. It had the conscious irregularity of hand-made things, so that there could never be an exact duplicate. It varied somewhat in thickness from end to end, and was a little bowed and twisted; when Alda lifted it and set the mouthpiece to his lips the double pipe, projecting some fifteen inches above his head, curved very slightly over his left shoulder. He held it with his left hand at waist level, and fingered below at the full stretch of his right arm; and round the finger-holes carved and painted mountain boys circled, dancing.

A gust of breathy, rustling notes came cascading out of the pipe, twining and shaking downwards in an improvised flourish, to settle deeply and sonorously into a slow, plaintive tune. It was hardly louder here, but for the reverberations from the walls, than when they had heard it descending from the hills beyond the col, through a couple of miles of mountain air.

"This is my rifle," said Alda, taking his lips from the mouthpiece and turning the pipe gently in his hands. "We call it the *fujara*—not very portable, and a little ponderous to play, because of all the over-blowing, but the queen of the pipes, all the same. The nearest thing to a gun I've ever possessed, or am ever likely to. Did you never hear it, down in the valley?"

"We heard it, yes." Dominic stretched out his hand and took the pipe, fascinated. The wood was silken smooth under his fingers. The little bandits, axes brandished above their heads, leaped like deer, legs doubled under them. "But we didn't know what it looked like, we'd never seen one. How could we guess?" He fitted his fingers to the holes, and held the instrument against him; and it hung lightly enough, for all its bulk. "What did you call it? A *fujara*? It's beautifully made."

"My great-grandfather made it. For a *fujara* it's on the small side, most of them run close to two metres." He laid it back carefully in its corner, cushioned by the folds of the heavy cloak.

"So it was you," said Dominic. "I wasn't imagining things, you *did* play 'Bushes and Briars'."

"Very probably. Was that what brought you up here after me?"

"Partly that. A musician who lived somewhere in these hills and knew English songs seemed a fair bet for Karol Alda. And by then I'd begun to think that maybe the whole business wasn't quite so obvious as it seemed, even before I knew your side of the story. I know now that you hadn't got anything to fear, or anything to hide, so why should you want to kill Welland? But you see, somebody else *has* got something to hide, somebody else *is* afraid. And I don't think we were wrong about what he's afraid of. He's killed once to keep your case from being dug up again and re-examined, and he may kill again for the same reason."

"Terrell's death was not murder," said Alda, considering him thoughtfully.

"No, I accept that. But it started Welland off on the same trail, and Welland's death *was* murder. And now that we know where you stand, and there isn't anything treasonable about co-operating, there's nothing to prevent Tossa and me from telling the whole truth. Will you come down to Pavol with me, and tell your part of it, too? Between us all, we ought to be able to clear up this case, and get Tossa out of trouble."

"I'm ready," said Alda. "We can go whenever you like."

: :   : :

Dominic was the first to set foot outside the open doorway, on the sunlit stone under the deep overhang.

There was a sharp, small crack. Something sheered into the weathered wall just in front of his face, and flying splinters stung his cheek. He clapped a startled hand to the place, and brought a smear of blood away on his fingers. And in the same instant Alda flung an arm about him and hoisted him bodily back into the hut in one heave, slamming the door to between them and the second bullet, as it thudded into the thick timbers where a split second before Dominic had been standing.

: :   : :

"I brought him here," said Dominic huskily, coming out of his moment of sickening shock with quickened senses. He wiped at his stinging cheek with the back of his hand, and stared almost disbelievingly at the minute smears of blood that resulted. " I got you to come down out of your clouds to help me, and now look what I've done! Led him straight to you."

" You don't know that. Does it matter, anyhow?" Alda drew breath cautiously, and looked the boy over in the warm wood-darkness within the closed door. All the lines of his face had sharpened and brightened, in what might have been merely tension, but looked strangely like pleasurable anticipation. He slid past Dominic to the small, single-paned window that let in light on this side of the hut.

" I do know. If he'd known exactly where to find you, he'd have come for you in the first place. It's *you* he wants suppressed. But he did know where *I* was, to a bit. All I've done is fetch you out of cover for him."

" No, you've done something much more useful, brought *him* out of cover. And if he was following you, why didn't he pick us both off while we were out on the talus?"

Dominic's mind was groping its way with increasing certainty through shadowy places. " He couldn't have been following me, not closely. But he knew where I'd gone. I think . . . I think he was betting on picking me up on the way back, but when I didn't go back promptly enough he came looking for me. He must have found the van. He'd know I was still up here, somewhere. If he'd arrived while we were exposed out there, we should both have had it. Therefore he didn't. He didn't reach these parts until we were inside here. And he didn't know there was anyone in here until he heard the *fujara*. What else could it be? That would be worth investigating, wouldn't it? He was looking for a musician. He only had to wait and see who emerged, to find out if he was wasting his time. Now he knows he wasn't. He knows we're both here. He's seen us."

" You're taking it for granted," said Alda equably, his

lean cheek flattened against the wall beside the dusty pane, " that he's someone who'll know me on sight."

" He'll know you. I'm sure."

" And that I'm critically dangerous to him. But I swear I know of no reason why I should be."

" I don't understand why, either, but I'm sure I'm right. Welland was killed because he was determined to find you, and he looked like succeeding. Tossa and I are marked down because Welland might have told us what he knew. But you're at the heart of it. There's something in your past, in your connection with England, that can ruin somebody, and if he can silence you, the urgency's over. And I brought you and pinned you here for him !"

" Up to now," said Alda, " we are still alive. If he knows where we are, let's see if we can find out where he is. He must be on this side, since he has the doorway neatly covered." He reached a hand out of shelter to rub away the dust from the window-pane. There was no shot. " The sun probably reflects from the glass, it's directly on it. So much the better. Come here ! "

Dominic came, slipping along the wall and pressing intently at his shoulder, to peer out at the pale corduroy hillside curving away from them round the side of the bowl, until it reached the talus. He looked down the broken, scoured, almost grassless fall below to the bottom of the basin, and again up from the talus by the bare, polished funnel to where the level of firm rock conducted the path across it. The whole bowl seemed, at first glance, to be void of cover, but when he considered it in more detail there was scattered and meagre cover everywhere.

" I am supposed," said Alda serenely in his ear, " to be somewhat of a prodigy at mathematics. Let's see how precisely I can calculate. I don't propose to open the door again simply to try and examine the bullet-hole, but I estimate that he was shooting obliquely into the doorway. The angle I should judge to be something like thirty degrees. And he's certainly on a higher level than we are. The scar makes things easier—at least we can write off the areas where he can't possibly be." He was silent for a moment, his eyes roaming the exposed stretch of country intently, his hand on Dominic's shoulder. "I make him approximately on the level of the rock path up there. Draw a line along from the distant end of it, say twenty yards. Somewhere within ten yards above or below that line, according to my estimate, he should be. You have that area fixed?"

"Yes." There were low clumps of bushes there, and some irregularities in the folded ground; it looked a possible hide.

"Keep it fixed. Watch for the slightest movement there, when I give you the word. I'll see if I can draw him."

It was extraordinary; his voice sounded gay, his step was elastic, there was no doubting his pleasure now. Dominic, faithfully fixing the oblong of ground he had marked down, longed to turn and look at his companion. Maybe it was true that they were all born Janosíks, venturers by instinct, even the artists.

"A hat wouldn't be convincing," mused Alda cheerfully, somewhere behind him. "A shirt-sleeve, perhaps. You're ready?"

"I'm ready," he said huskily, his eyes already aching with concentration.

The shot made him leap and shrink inside his skin all the more violently because he was waiting for it with so much passion. Alda made a small, echoing sound on the heels of the impact, half hiss, half laugh, drawing in breath through his teeth. And in the low bushes at the very edge of the rock path, that were quivering faintly and constantly in the breeze, there was a sudden tiny convulsion for which the wind was not responsible.

"He's there! I've got him!" He could turn his head now, and he did, in a frenzy of anxiety, reaching a hand for Alda's arm as he came slipping back to him. "You're all right? He didn't touch you?"

"I'm all right." He was laughing to himself, a small, inward rhythm like a cat purring. "Where was he?"

"Right at the edge of the scar, a yard or so above the

path. It's all still there now, but I'm sure. I saw him move. Only he may not stay there," he said, his heart contracting ominously. " If we don't return his fire soon, he'll know we're unarmed. If once he gets the idea, he can come down at leisure and get us. We'd have to cross open ground every way if we ran for it." He had got his companion into this, and he must get him out. " Even if we could kid him we had a gun here," he said, " we might keep him frozen where he is."

And suddenly it occurred to him that they were not totally defenceless. One man with a gun here on the door side of the hut, and the enemy would have to keep cover, and fix his attention upon that danger. There was the window at the back, and a sporting chance of reaching cover from it, and escaping into the valley. That fellow up there couldn't look everywhere at once.

He turned his head again and looked at Alda, who was scanning the rifleman's hide with narrowed, eager eyes.

" Would you mind terribly if I borrowed your *fujara*?"

Alda started, shortened his ardent stare, and looked with amusement and delight at his ally. He was very quick on the uptake.

" You won't take in a Slovak that way," he warned indulgently.

" No, I know that," acknowledged Dominic, gazing back at him with eyes wide and steady. " But I haven't got to— have I?"

They understood each other perfectly. In some incomprehensible way they had borrowed from each other, and even words had become almost superfluous, so companionably did their minds confer.

" You know the lie of the land here better than I do. You speak the language, I don't. And you're the more essential witness now. I don't understand why, either, but you are. Let me hold his fire here, and you get out by the window and run for help. I'm awfully sorry," said Dominic, picking his words as fastidiously as a drunk in his anxiety, " to be cornering the safe job for myself, but it's quicker and easier this way. If you'll let me try to use the *fujara* for camouflage, I shall be safe enough. He won't dare rush me, if he thinks I have a gun."

It was perhaps the most important speech of his life, up to that moment, and he had to get it right. He licked sweat from his lips. All that mattered now was Tossa, safe for a little while in Ondrejov's care, and safe for ever, even from baseless regrets for that bird-of-prey, her stepfather, once Karol Alda reached Liptovsky Pavol.

There was a brief and pregnant silence; then Alda said, with a soft ripple of contented laughter: " A good idea! All right, I'll go. Take the *fujara.*"

Dominic didn't at first recognise the chill that budded so curiously in his heart. It wasn't fear; he was too excited to be afraid. Fear comes more leisurely and deliberately, and grips the corner of your consciousness that isn't keyed up to resist it. It was a full minute before he recognised it as disappointment. He had what he'd wanted, but somehow he hadn't expected to get it so easily, without question. He took the *fujara* in his hands, the smooth, pale, polished, painted wonder that had to do duty for a gun.

" Say when you're ready, and I'll try to cover you."

He heard the harsh sound of a rusty hasp yielding, the creak of the window-frame.

"When you like. I'm ready."

" Good! Now!"

Dominic opened the door violently, took one rapid step out upon the stone, and on the instant recoiled, stiffening against the jamb. The shot smacked with unnerving aplomb into the opposite door-post; he stared at the hole in dreadful fascination. At least he knew the angle now. If the marksman had been at the opposite end of the rock crossing, Dominic Felse would have been as good as dead.

Vaguely, at the back of his mind, he heard the soft thud of Alda's feet on the ground outside the window, and their light, fleet running. This was the most desperate of all the moments left to him. He might have a long siege to withstand, but Karol Alda must get away safely. Dominic skinned off his red sweater, and swung it before him across the threshold.

Five! Another hole in the timbers of the wall, terrifyingly close, and two holes through his sweater at the shoulder. He leaned against the jamb of the door, and his knees felt like jelly. How many shots could there be in the magazine? And all he was armed with was a *fujara*; a beautiful, strange, mysterious musical instrument, the antithesis of every known instrument for killing, a whispering pipe that made itself heard over ten miles of country like a melody dreamed rather than heard, and other-worldly even in a dream.

The running footsteps were quite lost now. He strained his ears, and could hear nothing but the last light sighing of the wind under the eaves of the hut.

He pushed the door to carefully, leaving only a narrow chink open; and tenderly he raised his long weapon, and slid it forward through the crack, drawing a bead upon the bushes at the end of the rock path.

After that there was silence. Even the wind had dropped in the height of the afternoon hush.

:   :   :   :

He watched the clump of bushes where the enemy lay hidden, and lost count of time. He had no attention to spare for any other spot in all that arena of grass and rock and scree. That was why he failed to see Karol Alda until he lay some twenty yards above and behind the rifleman in the bushes, at the rim of the circle round which Dominic's feverish attention patrolled steadily and dutifully, all senses at strain. He froze, helpless and appalled.

So that was why Alda had accepted his rôle with such deceptive placidity, Alda with his adventurer's face and his far-sighted eyes, the bandit-artist out of the lawless past, with the old brigand-songs ready on his tongue. He had never had the slightest intention of going for help. He was patiently, calmly, happily circling round above his enemy, unarmed as he was, dropping now into the perimeter of Dominic's charmed circle, behind the gunman in the bushes.

And there was nothing, nothing at all, that Dominic could do to help him. Except, perhaps, show himself again outside the door, and that he could hardly do with conviction until the crucial moment. It couldn't go on being convincing indefinitely, he had to save it as his trump-card. He held his breath, watching. The muzzle of the *fujara* sagged a little, and he jerked it back guiltily, his heart lurching and recovering in an instant.

How could he ever have thought that a man like Karol Alda would leave the sticky end to him? He might have known. He should have known.

The sun was still high, and shadows still short and black. There was only one way of moving in undetected from the south-west, and that was flat to the ground. Alda had a gift for this game, Dominic had to grant him that. He must have made a large circle to reach the place of vantage where he now lay. From the hut he looked as obtrusive as a lizard spread out in the heat on a sunlit wall, though he had rolled up the wide white sleeves of his shirt to his sunburned shoulders; but from where the enemy lay, equally flat to the ground in his thicket of gnarled bushes, Alda would be quite invisible. From here, too, cover looked pitifully thin between them; but he knew to his comfort that there was more of it than there seemed.

But the one man had a gun, and the other had only his hands, and the odds were crazy. He shouldn't have done it. He should have made off down the valley to get help, as fast as he could. Dominic gnawed his knuckles and dripped sweat in an agony of helplessness. Even if he propped up the *fujara* here and made a run for it from the rear window now, he couldn't possibly reach either the nearest cottage or Alda in time to affect the issue. All he could do was stare until his eyes glazed, and wait for the single decisive moment when he ought to draw the enemy's fire again. It might all depend on his timing yet.

Another yard gained. Dominic caught the rapid, smooth movement as Alda flowed through the grass. Fifteen yards

now between them, not more, and this afternoon hush over
everything, not even a breath of wind to rustle the bushes
and cover his advance. Nobody could be so silent as to leave
that stillness undisturbed at only a few yards distance. The
mystery was how he had got so close without betraying
himself.

The bushes stirred stealthily, up there at the edge of the
scar. A streak of brown slid out of cover beneath the silver-
green branches, articulated, deliberate, grotesque, a man's
body. The man with the rifle had caught that last movement, and awakened to the near and perilous presence of
his stalker. He was leaving his hide, slithering downhill flat
on his belly, with the clump of bushes between him and his
pursuer, feeling his way backwards to the edge of the rock
slide, and cautiously over it.

Of course! He didn't know whether his antagonist was
armed or not, and he was taking no chances. He wanted
rock, not bushes, between himself and Alda. He was easing
himself down to a tenable hold, some five feet or so below
the edge, where the stray boulders that fringed the broken
ground would cover him.

The distant figure, featureless and anonymous, had
turned its back now on the hut below, and paid no attention when Dominic, grasping with a revulsion of horror
what was to come, flung the door wide and ran out into
the open. He was no longer interested in any target but the
unseen enemy in the grass above him, closing in coolly and
patiently on the abandoned bushes, and gathering himself
now for the final long leap downhill.

Dominic made a trumpet of his hands and yelled wildly
aloft. And at the same moment Alda made his leap, beautifully and vainly gauged to drop him upon the very spot
from which the other man had so silently withdrawn.

The rifle, its barrel a bluish gleam in the sun, was already
braced and waiting for him. Dominic saw it flung up to
meet the hurtling body, felt the tension of the firing arm like
a pain transfixing his own flesh, and set his teeth and held
his breath, steeled for the shot. A small, distant, dry, bright

sound. The slopes took it up and tossed it among them in innumerable echoes, ripple on ripple, to die in the depths of the valley below.

The bushes threshed beneath Alda's falling body, swallowing him from sight. Dominic drew breath in a wail of despair, and stood staring numbly, so sick with his own impotence that he saw what happened next only as an illogical sequence experienced in a dream, and for several seconds could make no sense of it in this disastrous daylight world.

The man braced on the rough rim of the rock chute hung quite still for a long moment. Then slowly his arms sank and spread apart, and the rifle slithered from his hold, and drifted away from him almost languidly, to lodge in a tuft of grass ten feet below, and hang there gently rocking. His outspread hands clutched at the rock and the thinning soil beneath him, and found no purchase, or no strength to maintain their hold. His knees sagged gently under him, and his body began to slide, first with unbelievable slowness, then with gathering momentum, until it struck a projecting knuckle of rock, and was flung abruptly outwards towards the centre of the chute. It struck again, and rebounded, and came spinning and turning and bouncing downwards like a stone.

In the dwarf bushes above, Karol Alda gathered himself up nimbly, and slid hastily down the few yards to where the rock path began. He reached the edge just in time to see the rag-doll form strike the piled stones of the talus on the ledge below. A sudden convulsion shuddered through the whole laborious erection, running like a ripple from the shock, outward to either end. Particles of stone shifted, toppled, re-settled, and set their new neighbours shuddering in their turn. Then, with a sudden grinding roar, the whole unstable mass burst from its shaky moorings and exploded violently outwards over the valley, spitting rocks like chaff, and hurtled down with the body, in an earth-shaking thunder and a cloud of pallid dust, into the bottom of the bowl.

Chapter 11

THE MAN WHO FAILED TO ARRIVE

Down from the recesses of the northerly col Ondrejov came bouncing and rolling, that lumpy elderly body of his marvellously deft and rapid in movement, his rifle bumping vigorously at his hip as he ran. Hard on his heels came Miroslav Zachar, still in his leather motor-cycling jacket, and sweating profusely, and two young policemen in uniform. They descended upon the hut, where Dominic stood dazed and appalled, staring down into the cauldron below him, from which a thick, choking smoke of dust rose, and the last muted rumblings of the thunder.

Ondrejov turned him about by the shoulders, looked him over for damage, and found nothing worse than a scratched cheek.

"Well for you two," he bellowed, clouting him boisterously behind in his relief, "that I've kept my hand in with a rifle. And well for you I had Mirek on your trail. He was waiting for you below, and you never came. You cost him a fine hunt before he found the van, and a fine fright I got when he rang up to tell me. If you youngsters would only do as you're told! I had the road well covered for your sake, but we had to reorganise in a hurry. There'll be two of us on their way up the valley now, and the rest of us came over the quickest way from Král's inn. And lucky for you the first shot gave us our bearings. You're all right?"

"Yes. Thank you! I'm all right," said Dominic, still staring down into the boiling eddies of dust below, beneath which the wreckage of the talus still slid and settled with sluggish, sated movements. He thought of a body buffeted and ground and slashed in that titanic disintegration, and the body became live, and his own. He would never play with those things again! He felt sick, but he was alive. For the moment that was all he could feel, and it was enough.

"Mr. Alda . . ." he said. His tongue was slow and stupid, and his mouth dry with dust. "Mr. Veselsky, I mean. . . ."

"Mr. Veselsky is on his way down, look! Like one of his own goats! Does he look damaged? *Nie*, there was only one shot—mine."

Alda was dropping down the grass slope on the far side of the scar in long, sure-footed bounds, balanced like a dancer. They saw that he carried a rifle in his hands.

"Good!" said Ondrejov. "The gun at least we have, if we can't have the man." He laid his arm warmly about Dominic's shoulders, and turned him towards the descent into the bowl. "Come on, let's go down. Let's see what we have there."

What they had was a wilderness, a new desolation. They foregathered in silence in the safe, hollowed heart of the bowl, where nothing could fall any farther, and ranged the scattered fringes of a desert of tumbled stones, through a pall of acrid dust that still silted down thickly on every blade of grass between the rocks, until there was no green left. Somewhere under those piled cairns the body of Robert Welland's murderer was buried.

"There won't be much to identify," said Ondrejov grimly, "but I suppose we shall have to dig him out. We shall need heavy equipment on the job. You didn't, by any chance, get a proper look at him?"

"No, nothing. I saw only the end of his fall."

"And we had no field-glasses. No telescopic sights, not even a diopter. Our best shots were covering the road." Ondrejov nodded sombrely, looking down at the rifle in his hands, on which the dust was settling pale and fine as talc. "He had, though. A Zbrojovka Brno gun, of course. ZKM 581 small-calibre rifle. Automatic. Light to carry, not too bulky to hide, and a man could run into them by the thousand here. That tells us nothing till we find out who applied for the permit to buy it. As we shall." He shook himself like an experienced old dog making ready for action, and turned towards the downhill path, coughing. " Let's get back where we can breathe. We'll work this out in Pavol."

" Then we still don't know who he is," said Dominic, swept along in Ondrejov's arm, shaky with reaction now.

Ondrejov hoisted an eloquent shoulder. " We soon shall. We're in no hurry now." He looked back once, briefly, at the murky desolation where the murderer lay buried. " Neither is he," he said laconically. " Even for him, the emergency's over."

: :   : :

" I'm officially off-duty," said Ondrejov smugly, " but as Major Kriebel is at Liptovsky Mikulás, examining Mr. Welland's baggage at his hotel there, and enquiring into his movements, I shall take the liberty of presiding until he returns."

And he did, and the wires hummed. First, the salvage operations in Zbojská Dolina; then a dutiful call, naturally, to Major Kriebel, so worded that he would, with luck, feel it incumbent upon him, in defence of his dignity, to go to survey the devastation in the valley before he came back to Pavol; and lastly, calls to the two hotels at Mikulás where Freeling, Blagrove and Sir Broughton Phelps had installed themselves, and across the square to the Slovan, where Paul Newcombe had taken a room. None of them was actually in his hotel to be contacted personally, which was hardly surprising on a lovely August afternoon; it was a question of leaving a message in each case, asking them all to report at Ondrejov's office, in person or by telephone, as soon as possible.

That done, Ondrejov assembled his cast for the last act, the Mather twins from their forlorn and fruitless councils of war at the Slovan, Tossa from a long and blissful sleep on her solitary cot downstairs. And they all talked at last, fully and freely.

After that, Ondrejov talked.

: :   : :

" When Mr. Terrell was found dead," he said, " I was already in possession of the facts about that death, but not of the background. I therefore knew from the beginning that this was not a case of murder. But there were certain curious features about it that interested me. And when you, Miss Barber, applied for a visa, with your friends, the authorities, who were also on the alert, contacted me. We supplied you with Mirek as an escort, and waited to see what would follow. And it was known to me, before the death of Mr. Welland brought things into the open, that you were making enquiries about your stepfather's movements. Movements which we already knew, but to which your anxiety gave significance. You even uncovered some points which were not known to us. For instance, at the Hotel Sokolie—you remember the waiter who spoke English? He was a very worried man, Miss Barber, very worried. He had thought nothing of the small matter of the card-game, and the paper on which Ivo Martínek kept the score, until you became excited about it."

Tossa, refreshed and radiant, sat by Dominic's side, and smiled back at Ondrejov with all her heart. She had never looked younger, and never in Dominic's experience half so light-hearted. She was clear of suspicion, clear even of her suspicions of herself. Terrell had not been a hero or a patriot, but only an ambitious schemer bent on climbing in his profession, if necessary over other people's faces. She was free of him, she had her life back fresh and new, and she had Dominic tightly by the hand. She knew now, though imperfectly, how nearly she had lost him.

"Naturally I questioned the Martíneks about that incident; so already I had a picture of another kind of case, with its roots somewhere in the past, even before Mr. Welland was killed. I knew from Mr. Veselsky—shall I call him Mr. Alda, for our purposes?—I knew from Mr. Alda that he had known Terrell, and worked in the same enterprise with him in England. I knew from your activities that you suspected Terrell had been hunting for someone or something in the neighbourhood of Zbojská Dolina, and I knew from Ivo the nature of the lead he—and you after him—had found. Of Welland I knew only that he had known Terrell, and that he, too, was returning with marked persistence to the place where Terrell had died, also plainly in search of something there. It was as evident to me as it was to you that every thread led into the heart of that one valley, and that the person to whom all those threads were leading must be Mr. Alda. The man who had known and worked with Terrell, and reported his death, the man who had an English past of some importance. Which, naturally, we, too, investigated.

" Now you, Miss Barber, have been so kind as to fill in all the gaps. It is very lucky for me, that Mr. Welland was forced by circumstances to confide in you. I had not this detailed knowledge then, but I had enough to show me that certain persons, *all English*, were very much interested in locating Mr. Alda, and that after the death of the first of them those of you who were continuing the search obviously held that same death to be murder. I knew it was not; but it was interesting to think that there was somewhere, known to someone, a reason why it *could* have been murder. And the second death *was* murder. I was not altogether prepared for that, never having taken it quite seriously. Your secret agent game became real, quite suddenly, because it appeared there *was* someone who was desperate to prevent you from finding Mr. Alda, someone who had killed and would kill again to keep the facts about his departure from England from being re-examined, or the case re-opened in any way.

" But where I had the advantage of you, of course, was in knowing beforehand that it *could not* be Mr. Alda himself. We preserve his quietness here, but that is not the same thing as keeping his secrets. He lives a life in which not even an Englishman could find anything underhand or controversial, he has nothing to hide and nothing to fear, and he would not care how many English people came investigating him, provided they didn't hinder his work. For the same reasons, *it could not be any other Czech or Slovak*, official or unofficial."

He had reached this point, when there was a knock on the outer door. Mirek got up from his place and looked enquiringly at his chief.

"Let him in," said Ondrejov, settling his solid body more complacently in his wooden arm-chair, and his chin more contentedly into his chest. "Let's see who's the first."

Every head turned to watch the doorway; and into it, all the more belligerently for his considerable inward disquiet, marched Paul Newcombe. He looked quietly round the circle, caught the excitement that burned in them all, and was alarmed, caught the glow and animation of Tossa's face, and was reassured. He halted, uncertain what to make of them.

"You left a message for me at the hotel. I was only out for a walk."

"Come in, Mr. Newcombe, come in. Mirek, find Mr. Newcombe a chair. You're just in time," pursued Ondrejov amiably, "to hear me conclude that the only person who could possibly have an interest in preventing an Englishman from finding Mr. Alda was someone connected with the circumstances in which he left England, someone who had gained by that case, and stood to lose by any reappraisal. In fact, *another Englishman*."

"I know absolutely nothing about this affair," Paul said loudly and aggressively, his bull head lowered in an instant. "I came from Vienna only because of Tossa, and that's all I care about. But I can account for every minute I've spent in this country."

"Ah, but you need not, Mr. Newcombe. Sit down, and be easy. You were never a very likely suspect. Now if it had been Terrell's murder, I might have wondered. . . . But in any case you have accounted for yourself quite adequately," said Ondrejov, grinning like a happy demon, "simply by being here—and alive."

: :   : :

"We have, then, our hypothetical Englishman. Can we give him any distinguishing features? A face? Not exactly, but an office or a status, perhaps, yes. He was connected with Mr. Alda's life and work in England. He gained by his leaving England. That, at least, was my theory.

"Now, thanks to Miss Barber, I know much more about Welland, how he came into the case, what his motives were, what sort of man he was. We know that he went to the Marrion Institute, and proposed that he, being here on the spot, should investigate what he believed to be Terrell's murder. He saw it as something they owed to the dead man, and to justice itself. Now I ask you, how could any of those in authority openly deprecate his zeal? They could not. In any case it seems he would not have agreed to drop his quest. I invite you to look closely at Mr. Welland, for I think he is worth it. There is every sign that he was a good, conscientious and honest man. And what follows? He would have insisted on investigating to the bitter end, and I think he would have made the truth known, no matter what that truth turned out to be. Which would not have suited X at all, for X alone knew exactly what was there to be uncovered."

"I hope," said Alda drily, "that you can make that good. For I tell you plainly, I am still in the dark."

"Well, let me theorise, it was all I could do then, and what Miss Barber has told me since fits in with my theory. As for you, you do not know only because you do not care. You will see!

"Given, then, a devoted avenger who means to know the truth, and will not be stopped by persuasion, and cannot for shame's sake be stopped by a prohibition, what is to be done? Use him! Let him find Alda, and then both he and Alda can be eliminated, and there's an end of it. Let him find Alda, yes, but only if it can be ensured that he shall report his whereabouts only in the right quarter. It seemed to me that X must be in a position to know all about that interview at the Institute, and also to give orders to Welland concerning this case, to say in effect: 'You will preserve absolute secrecy, reporting only to me', and be trusted and obeyed. ' Security ' is such a useful word, and can blanket so many personal meannesses.

" Now see what Miss Barber has told us about the last words Welland ever spoke to her. 'He couldn't have known. . . .' *He*? Obviously the expected he, the defecting scientist, the one who was thought to have things to hide, and had nothing, except his personal privacy. '—*no one else* knew. . . .' No one else but the one, or the ones, to whom he had already reported, the ones who had the right to know! He said it himself, and then he understood what it meant, and he cried : ' Impossible !' Impossible that his superior, the person, or one of the persons, for whom he was working, could also be his murderer. But he knew then that it was not impossible, that it was the truth.

" Such was my theory. And if this was true, then both Miss Barber and Mr. Felse were in danger after that death, simply because they had been present, and he might have confided something to them. Fortunately the circumstances made it possible for me to place Miss Barber in safety by holding her on suspicion. You would have made things much more difficult for me if you had told the truth the first time, but luckily you did not. And this, again, enabled me to inform the British Embassy that she was being held. You will surely understand how very curious I was to see exactly who would turn up to take charge of her. . . ."

It was not a knock this time, only the sudden, rather high-pitched, imperious English voice in the outer room. Ondrejov drew in a long, contented breath, knowing this one, and knowing him the most expendable.

" Another chair, Mirek." He rubbed his hands; how convenient that he had been able to secure all the time he wanted, simply by deflecting Major Kriebel's most avid attention to the salvage operations already under way in Zbojská Dolina. " Ah, Counsellor! Come in, come in! You received my message, then."

Charles Freeling closed the door after him with quiet precision, to show how perfectly he was in control of both his own reactions and the right manipulation of inanimate things.

" I should have been here earlier, but I had some trouble hiring a car. I preferred to come in person. Am I to take it that the matter is now cleared up, and Miss Barber no longer under restraint? Or is it intended to charge her?"

He took his stand, significantly, at her side, even laid his fingers delicately on her shoulder in reassurance. She did not even notice; she was clinging to Dominic's hand, but she was watching Ondrejov, with wonder and delight, her newly released and exuberant senses sharing his slightly mischievous but utterly human pleasure in his game.

" No, there will be no charge against her, Mr. Freeling. I am in process of uncovering the murderer of Mr. Welland, by elimination. I hope you will join us for the remainder of my exposition. We had reached the point of demonstrating that the murderer must be an Englishman, and one in a position of authority."

Freeling's eyebrows soared. Ondrejov was meant to notice them, and to appreciate, if it was not beyond him, the neat, satirical smile that accompanied their elevation. " I hope, I do hope, Lieutenant, that I am not your man?"

It was an attractive idea, in its way, and even just barely possible. Was it too much to conceive that a devoted and orthodox public servant might feel called upon to wipe out a less devoted and less orthodox one, in order to keep a discreditable case from being reviewed to England's embarrassment? It would have made a nice ending. A pity!

" You have good reason to hope so, Counsellor," said Ondrejov earnestly. " My man is already very, very dead."

: :   : :

" Well, as you know, there were four who ran gallantly to protect Miss Barber, and to argue eloquently that she should be released in their custody. I did not put her in that somewhat risky situation, naturally, since by then I was convinced that one of them had designs on her life. But I did, with planned safeguards, allow them a chance at Mr.

Felse. A chance which his own enterprise considerably complicated.

"We have now reduced our four to two. But we still have those two people to choose from, and the motives are surely taking form. Both of these men gained by ensuring Mr. Alda's disgrace. One of them, as I have learned, assisted Terrell in the compilation of the notorious dossier, was advanced in his profession as a result, and has now stepped into Terrell's shoes. The other became head of the Marrion Institute, a promotion which would have been unlikely if Mr. Alda had continued—I believe the word is 'clean'."

"It isn't enough," said Alda, suddenly and with authority. "Neither motive is strong enough for murder. For his whole career, for his reputation, a man might take such desperate measures. But my return now, even my vindication, would not have unseated anyone or disgraced anyone. Even if they all conspired to produce that dossier on me, and so quickly, all they had to do was sit tight and plead that they had acted throughout in good faith. They wouldn't be broken for that, either of them. Believe me, I know my England. They would be supported and covered to the limit, short of something like murder. I might get my reputation back, a little finger-marked. They wouldn't lose theirs."

"They do not discard their failures?" Ondrejov asked with interest.

"On the contrary, they promote them."

"And we are too quick to discard ours. Somewhere there must be a workable compromise." He scrubbed his chin with hard knuckles till the bristles rasped, and spared one twinkling glance to enjoy the lofty forbearance of Freeling's face. "Well, I accept your judgment. Then there must be more."

Dominic looked at Tossa, and she looked back at him with all her being open and happy behind her eyes, drawing him in. He closed his fingers on hers. "Tossa, do you remember, you told us at the Riavka that there were notebooks that vanished?" It was a detail she had forgotten to mention, in her haste, when rushing through her story to Ondrejov, an hour ago. " Tell them about that. What Welland told you."

She caught the glitter of his excitement without understanding it, and turned quickly to look at Alda. " Mr. Welland said they told him at the Marrion that you took all your papers away with you, when you went. All your notes, all your plans. . . . They told him the potential value was enormous, that you had planned work with you that could easily account for murder."

" Notes? Plans?" Alda met her eyes across the circle with a grey-blue stare of detached astonishment. " I never intended to leave. I went on holiday with a rucksack, and when I got back to Briançon I found myself already a traitor. I took nothing with me. What I stood up in, a change of shirt and underclothes, some music paper, and a little money. Nothing more."

" But you *had* projected work?" said Dominic intently. " Ideas that might have worked out and been worth a lot? You had them there, in the Institute?"

" Oh, yes, several. Some might have foundered. Most would have worked out. But I give you my word I left them there."

" Yet Robert Welland told me," said Tossa, her shining eyes fixed eagerly on Ondrejov, " that somebody there in the Institute—he didn't say who, but *one* of them—told him Mr. Alda had removed all his notes and papers. He said nobody knew it, except the Institute and the Ministry."

" And, don't you remember," Dominic took up just as ardently, appealing to Alda, " up there in your hut you told me about the crop-sprayer? The helicopter adaption? One of your ideas, put on the market by a commercial firm in France? How many years' work would it have taken, to put it into production?"

" Three. Four, perhaps, without me. It was a completely new engine, driving a re-designed three-blade rotor. I was glad to see it produced for ordinary, human uses. But someone else must have hit on it. Why should my design turn up in France?"

"Because it was safer than selling it in England," said Dominic. "Are you even sure it's the only one?"

"No," admitted Alda, startled. "How can I be sure? There could be others. I shouldn't care, I shouldn't think myself robbed. Better they should be used in the open market than filed for Institute modulations. They were always military! And we were not even a military establishment."

"And how many were there in all, in these notebooks?" asked Ondrejov. "How many such marketable projects?"

"It's hard to remember. Perhaps as many as nine or ten, at this same stage. Some others merely conceived and sketched out."

"A fortune!" said Ondrejov, and sat back with a long breath of fulfilment, spreading his hands peacefully on the table. "Is it enough to kill for now? To keep this from being uncovered? Would they have kept their jobs then? Their reputations? Either of them could have done it. You are gone, your papers are there. How easy, if the idea dawns in time, to make away with them, and say: You see, his flight was premeditated, he removed everything! Who would doubt it? Who would stop to wonder? It is a time of hysteria, press and public would make enough outcry to cover one man's orderly retreat with a stolen fortune under his arm. Either of them could have done it. Either of them was a natural repository for Welland's reports—one the Director, the other the Security Officer. Both of them turn up here. Either of them could have followed Welland to his rendezvous and shot him, and then returned from the scene, the one by plane back to Prague, the other to the White Carpathians—three or four hours by car, what is that?—in time to be fittingly surprised and distressed when he heard of Miss Barber's detention. Either of them could have acted on my hints, and followed Mr. Felse this morning, waiting to pick him off and make away with another possible witness. Mr. Blagrove could have hired a car in Mikulás—was that why *you* had difficulty, Counsellor?—Sir Broughton Phelps already had a car, hired in Bratislava. *One* of them had bought a ZKM 581 hunting rifle, with telescopic sights and the special sixteen-cartridge magazine. *Which?*"

The knock on the door and the abrupt burr of the telephone came at the same moment.

"Come in! shouted Ondrejov, and reached for the telephone. "*Ondrejov! No, islo to! Dobre, dobre!*" Hanging upon the telephone with held breath, and watching the door with snapping, sparkling blue eyes, he saw Adrian Blagrove enter the room, his long face wary, his long lips faintly disdainful, his aloof eyes more than a little defensive.

"*D'akujem, uz to viem,*" said Ondrejov gently to the telephone. "*Viem, kto to je.*" He hung up. "I know," he repeated in English, more to himself than to them, "I know now who he is."

He pushed the instrument away from him wearily but contentedly, to the length of his arm. "They have found the car from Bratislava, a little above the place where you hid your van, Mr. Felse, but better hidden. He had more cause to hide. And in the head of the valley they have also found Sir Broughton Phelps. What remains of him."

Chapter 12

THE MAN WITH THE *FUJARA*

The light in the room had mellowed into the fine, clear gold that came between the mountains at the onset of evening, and its clarity, sharp as wine, seemed to be the appropriate colour of the quietness that had descended after the young people were gone, marshalled away decisively by Karol Alda to his grandmother's farm by the southerly col; after

Paul Newcombe had accepted his polite but firm dismissal with a shrug, between offence and relief, and gone off to see about his return to Vienna next day; after the young constable had withdrawn to the outer room to clatter out the transcription of his notes on the typewriter, and Mirek Zachar had taken his Jawa and gone thankfully off-duty, with a light heart and his job completed.

" Lieutenant," Charles Freeling began very carefully and gravely, when the three of them were alone, " on behalf of my embassy I want to express our appreciation and admiration of the way you've handled this very difficult matter, and the consideration you showed towards these young people. I needn't tell you what a great shock this has been to us. We shall take up the matter of the Alda plans, of course. Clearly my country has done a great injustice to him, which ought to be set right. But it seems that he does not wish his case to be brought into prominence again at this late stage. For that I am grateful. We are none of us free agents, and absolute justice would seem to be a luxury we cannot always afford. At a time when technical and cultural co-operation between our countries is making such progress, is it worth while to allow old irregularities to obtrude? Publicity could do so much harm. We are being obliged to admit to a wrong. But since, after all, the man is dead. . . ."

Within one hour Sir Broughton Phelps had become " the man," an inconvenience, disowned, deprecated. This morning they would have been rolling out red carpets for him and listening enthusiastically to his fishing stories.

" Gentlemen," said Ondrejov, leaning back in his chair and spreading his great arms on the table with a gusty sigh, " I am merely a policeman, with a straightforward job to do, and I shall do it. I shall pass on the relevant information to Major Kriebel, and Major Kriebel will make his report in the proper quarter. After that it is out of our hands. But I think you need not worry too much. Here the newspapers do not go in for lurid reports of murders. And even if they did, you see the chief occasion for it is already lost. There will be no charge, there will be no trial. As you say, the man is dead."

Freeling looked at Blagrove, and Blagrove looked at Freeling, and visibly they bit on the reassurance, and found it sweet.

"And as for what you report and publish in England, provided you do no further injustice to Mr. Alda or to this country, that is no responsibility of mine. 'Sir Broughton Phelps Dies in Landslip in the Tatras'! It's all one to me," he said equably, "whether you see fit to add that he had a bullet-hole in him before he fell. It's enough that I was able to put it there, and in time. England is your own house, gentlemen," said Ondrejov. "Set it in order yourselves."

: :   : :

Outside the farmhouse windows looking westward, shadowed by the deep overhang of the eaves, the sky was smouldering in reds and yellows and livid greens, the flamboyant refractions from the dust of the talus, the funeral fires of Sir Broughton Phelps. In a high-backed wooden chair Mrs. Veselsky presided, bolt upright, eighty-three years old, and as clear-cut as the steely profile of Kriván, her lace cap and embroideries formal as a queen's regalia, her face proud and serene as she watched her grandson. Toddy and Christine, most readily adjusted, least involved, least changed of them all, hung enchanted over the grand piano that filled one end of the room, where Alda had spread out for them, on an embroidered shawl, the assembly of the pipes of Slovakia.

They passed from hand to hand, smoothing them and marvelling at their intricate decoration, the six-finger-holed labial pipe, the double pipe, the end-hole *koncovka*, the transverse folk flute, the children's reed-pipes, the ragman's whistle, the whole complex family from the toy *fanfárka* to the great *fujara*. Not the same they had left in the hut over the col; this one was at least six inches longer, and even more wonderfully painted and carved and inlaid.

"Well, anyhow," said Dominic, with his sore cheek against the cool tiles of the empty porcelain stove, Tossa close beside him in the shadowy corner, and peace on his eyelids like the palm of a warm hand, " you must admit that even when I got myself into a fight, I did find myself a genuinely defensive weapon."

Alda laughed, stroking the long golden flank of his pipe gently. He raised the mouthpiece to his lips and the *fujara* shook out its strange, shimmering banner of notes, forked and flying, as his fingers vibrated on the holes. He drew out the improvisation long and lovingly, brought it circling down like a skylark from the wild heights of air into the nest of one lingering, full, fluting note, out of which the melody rose plaintively and slowly, unfolding with such deliberation that they followed it like creatures bewitched, feeling their way, knowing it before they knew that they knew it.

Through bushes and through briars
I lately took my way. . . .

The incredible sunset was fading. To-morrow there would be nothing left but the transient layer of dust on the stones in Zbojská Dolina, waiting for the first cleansing rain, the new rock town in the bottom of the bowl, and the almost-empty saucer at the foot of the scar. But there would still be the recurring springs, and the chestnut goats, and this music; as long as anything remained, these would remain.

Sometimes I am uneasy
And troubled in my mind. . . .

No, that belonged to the bushes and briars of old distress. Tossa's mind, newly adult, embraced its responsibilities with awe but without fear. Chloe Terrell would be getting back from Slovakia a new daughter, out of her power, wiser, older, larger than she.

Sometimes I think I'll go to my love
And tell to . . . her . . . my mind.

But not yet, not here, not in this land, where they had bumped full tilt into death together, and she had been startled into mistaking a moment's human warmth and solidarity for something rarer and more personal. He mustn't touch her now, however much he longed to. She was hardly out of her chrysalis, she had to have time to try her wings.

> *But if I should go to my love,*
> *My love he will say nay. . . .*

He'd almost forgotten that this was really a woman speaking, but Tossa had remembered it. She was singing the words in her husky whisper, close beside him, and her hand, hidden in the shadowy corner between them, felt for his hand, and closed on it warmly.

> *" If I show to him my boldness*
> *He'll ne'er love me again."*

There was no urgency now, and no danger; and yet when he turned his head and saw her smiling at him in the dimming light, her eyes looked to him just as they had looked before she left him in the chapel, only to wait for him, against orders, at the edge of the trees : clear, assured, roused and glad.

" Wouldn't it be a marvellous world," said Tossa, staring ahead into a future as uncertain and dangerous as the future had always been, and yet as attractive and promising, " where we could go straight up to one another and ask what we wanted to know? Where all the secret formulae turned out to be songs, and all the rifles were *fujaras*!"